RF
LARGE PRINT

Awarded for excellence in public service
Dumfries and Galloway
Libraries, Information and Archives

Dumfries and Galloway
L I B R A R I E S
Information and Archives

Central Support Unit: Catherine Street Dumfries DG1 1JB
tel: 01387 253820   fax: 01387 260294   e-mail: libs&i@dumgal.gov.uk

24 HOUR LOAN RENEWAL BY PHONE AT LO-CALL RATE - 0845 2748080
OR ON OUR WEBSITE - WWW.DUMGAL.GOV.UK/LIA

SAFE HARBOUR

When Adam Hawthorne with his sharp suit and devastating looks drives into the town of Seaport, Cassandra knows he's dangerous. Not only do his plans threaten to ruin her successful harbourside restaurant, but also Adam stirs painful memories she'd rather forget. When Cassandra's sister Ellie turns up, in trouble as usual, Cassandra needs all her considerable strength to cope. But will discovering dark secrets from Adam's past change Cassandra's future? And will he be her saviour or her downfall?

CARA COOPER

SAFE HARBOUR

Complete and Unabridged

LINFORD
Leicester

First published in Great Britain in 2008

First Linford Edition
published 2009

British Library CIP Data

Cooper, Cara
   Safe harbour.—Large print ed.—
Linford romance library
1. Love stories
2. Large type books
I. Title
823.9'2 [F]

ISBN 978–1–84782–562–9

Published by
F. A. Thorpe (Publishing)
Anstey, Leicestershire

Set by Words & Graphics Ltd.
Anstey, Leicestershire
Printed and bound in Great Britain by
T. J. International Ltd., Padstow, Cornwall

This book is printed on acid-free paper

A Stranger In Town

Cassandra Waverley stood at the window of her small harbourside restaurant. If the man across the street had noticed her watching him, then he wasn't letting on. She bit her thumbnail and shifted uneasily from one foot to the other.

'He's been out there for forty minutes,' she said to her waitress, Megan. 'Someone should go and ask him what he's up to.'

Megan peered at the stranger standing across the road while she carried on with her task of rolling up sets of cutlery in paper napkins.

'If you're so concerned then you should go and ask him yourself.'

'That's exactly what I'd like to do but, unfortunately, I don't own the street so I can't go and accost people who are hanging around in it and demand to know what they're up to.'

Cassandra was aware that her reaction to the chap across the street was a bit over the top, but she did think his behaviour was rather odd.

'Actually, he's kind of yummy, don't you think?' commented Megan.

Exasperation rang in Cassandra's voice. 'How can you think that a man with stony black eyes and a cold stare, who's probably loitering with intent, is yummy? I'd say he looks dodgy.'

Megan stopped what she was doing and put her head to one side, considering. 'I'd say he looks dangerous rather than dodgy. Wonderfully dangerous, in a thrilling sort of way. I'd take bets this sleepy old town hasn't seen a man so dangerous-looking since there were pirates in the harbour.'

'Yup, and the pirates were chased away because nobody wanted their sort round here. What on earth do you think he's up to?'

Cassandra could feel her chest tightening with tension.

Megan abandoned the cutlery and went to join her boss by the window. 'Maybe he's a tourist?' she ventured.

'On his own, wearing a suit and pacing backwards and forwards? I don't think so. He's casing the joint in some way.'

'Casing the joint!' Megan laughed. 'You've been watching too many gangster movies.'

'Well, there are a couple of new antiques places opened around the corner — he might be sussing them out.'

'You know what I think?' said Megan, taking a bundle of napkins and sitting down at a table to resume her task of wrapping a knife, fork and spoon in each one.

'No. What do you think?' asked Cassandra, all ears.

'I think you've got too fertile an imagination.' Megan placed a rolled-up napkin in a large earthenware jug and prepared to start the next one.

'I'm only doing my bit towards

protecting the neighbourhood.'

Cassandra ran her hand along the crystals which dangled from silver threads in front of the window. The movement threw rainbows round the restaurant walls from the early morning sun.

'And protecting myself.'

'Are they part of your protection?' Megan pointed to the dancing glass crystals.

'Of course they are. They energise the Chi currents which promote harmony and happiness. Perhaps they'll chase away that burglar across the street.'

Megan snorted. 'If he really is some sort of crook, it'll take a lot more than a few sparkly crystals and you frowning at him to see him off.' She didn't know anything about all that mystical Chinese stuff but she knew that since Cassandra had bought and done up the restaurant, it did have an extraordinarily peaceful feeling about it.

Cassandra wandered over to the bar

at the back of the restaurant. Megan might not be bothered by the stranger, but then *she* didn't own the Feng Shui restaurant. *She* hadn't staked her whole future in it, along with virtually every penny she had.

Taking a pair of secateurs out of a drawer, Cassandra marched across to the door, a determined look on her face.

'Crikey, you're not planning to attack him with those, are you?'

'Very funny. I'm going out to pick some fresh flowers for the tables and to let him know that I've seen him.'

'I'll bet that'll set him quaking in his shoes.'

'You may laugh, but letting them know they've been observed can be enough to deter some criminals.'

★   ★   ★

She stepped out into the spring sunshine brandishing her secateurs.

The stranger was standing on the

corner now, writing in a small note-book. She glared at him, getting ever more annoyed as he studiously concen-trated on his notes, stubbornly failing to look towards her. She snipped at the cloud of scented philadelphus which grew in the tiny garden at the front of the restaurant, and selected the longest-stemmed white roses from the climber which grew around the door.

She felt uneasy with her back turned towards him. She glanced around quickly and caught him looking across at her restaurant again. What was he up to?

The tourist season hadn't yet started in the sleepy seaside town of Seaport, and unfamiliar faces stuck out like sore thumbs.

Then Cassandra's next door neigh-bour, Jasper Eames, came ambling out from his bookshop to stand, stretching and yawning, on his doorstep. Jasper was one of those dishevelled men who looked like a perpetual schoolboy — he even had ink stains on his fingers.

'Good morning.' He grinned at her. 'You're a sight for sore eyes for a man who's been staring at accounts all morning.'

'Hi, Jasper. Your accounts wouldn't take half as long if you did them on a computer. You just need the correct software. I offered to show you how.'

'No, thanks. I'll stick with the slow torture of doing them with good old-fashioned pen and paper. Computers and I don't get on.'

'You're probably right. Any man who can run a business for as long as you have without even owning a mobile phone is probably a lost cause where modern technology is concerned. Jasper, what do you think that guy can be up to across the street? He's been prowling about for ages.'

'Can't say I've noticed him,' answered Jasper. 'You're the only one I really notice around here. You're looking extraordinarily nice today, I must say.'

'Thanks for the compliment, but you

must have noticed him. He's been hanging around for ages.'

'He's just an early tourist, I guess. Nice flowers,' he said, nodding to the bunch in her hand.

'Here.' She offered him some of the blooms. 'Have a rose for your desk.'

'Don't mind if I do, although it should be the other way around. I should be offering you flowers.'

'Well, don't you go getting any bright ideas. I'm far too busy running a business to take time out to flirt with you.'

'You say the sweetest things, Cassandra.' Jasper ran his fingers through his hair in a vain attempt to look as if he actually cared about his appearance, and focussed on the stranger for the first time. 'I reckon he could be a property developer. Isn't that a measuring device he's got in his hand?'

Cassandra's hand dropped to her side, and the secateurs nearly fell from her grasp. 'Property developer?' she breathed, prickles of anxiety running up her spine. She'd given up a high-powered job in London to move to the peace and quiet of Seaport, and she didn't want the town spoiled. 'Oh heavens, I hope not.'

'Why not? We could do with a few luxury flats hereabouts to smarten the place up a bit. Have you seen that new development along the beach where the Old Ship Inn used to be? Really smart it is. Brand new flats, all glass and steel with posh balconies looking out over the sea. I'd buy one myself if I had the money.'

'But most of the properties along this street are listed buildings. I was counting on all this staying as it is. I love it here.'

'That's because you're an incomer. You have a romantic view of the area. Not like those of us who were born here. The old place could do with a bit of a shake-up. Anyway, much as I'd like to stand here and look at you all day, I have to open up if I'm going to make a living.'

With that, he ambled back into his shop and flipped the *CLOSED* sign to *OPEN*, and Cassandra shot back inside the restaurant and grabbed her black jacket.

'Going somewhere?' enquired Megan.

'Jasper thinks that chap across the street's a property developer. If he is, I'm going out there to give him a piece of my mind. These people,' she snapped, 'come to small, quiet places like this because they *are* small and quiet, and then they turn them into a yuppiefied version of what I've come here to get away from.'

She yanked her long hair out of her jacket and tied it back into the severest ponytail she could manage.

'Very businesslike.' Megan looked up. 'Go get him, Cassandra.'

★   ★   ★

Cassandra marched out to meet her adversary. With her lips pursed and her arms rigid at her side, she strode up

10

to the stranger and tapped him on the shoulder.

'Yes?' He turned around and she realised he was even taller than he'd looked from a distance. Imposing was the word which immediately sprang to mind. Imposing and good-looking. Very good-looking.

But to heck with his looks, she thought, as she opened her mouth to speak . . . then suddenly, standing there in the sunshine in the quiet little English street, she realised how absurd it was to go accosting complete strangers with mad ideas about robbers and dastardly property developers. Quite frankly, when it came to it, Cassandra Waverley suddenly felt extremely silly and totally lost her bottle.

'I . . . I just wondered if you were lost,' she said in a quiet voice.

He looked down at her like a headmaster regarding an errant child. His dark eyes betrayed nothing, and his jawline was set firm and immobile.

'This is Seaport, isn't it?'

11

'Yes.' All her fight had been replaced by meekness.

'And this is Park Street, isn't it?'

'Yes,' she squeaked.

'Then, no, I'm not lost. Are you?'

He must have noticed her watching him from the window of The Feng Shui, and he must have seen her picking flowers from the restaurant's garden in a very proprietorial way, so his question was obviously intended as a rather rude rebuff.

She held up her chin. 'I was just trying to be helpful.'

'Were you now?' His statement was less a question and more a challenge to her to defend herself on a charge of nosiness in the first degree.

'Of course. We locals like to be helpful to tourists.'

'Well, that must be very comforting to tourists.'

She took a second to study him. He was incredibly well-dressed. His expensive suit, perfectly cut, had probably been made for him.

She waited for him to continue, with a hopeful look in her eyes. Waited for him to give her some clue as to what he was up to. And the longer she waited, the more embarrassing it became. He was not going to play her game, and if there was one thing Cassandra couldn't abide, it was silence. She had to fill the space.

'It's a beautiful day, isn't it?'

'It's OK.'

Those two words sounded so obviously dismissive that she felt herself fold up inside with embarrassment. If only she hadn't started this. If only she'd curbed her stupid imagination and left him alone, she wouldn't now be standing there with Megan watching, on tenterhooks, from the restaurant, and with Jasper Eames frowning at her from behind his desk in the bookshop window.

That was the trouble with small places like Seaport, everybody was interested in everybody else's business.

Funny, she thought, but before she'd

come here, when she was working at the bank in London, she would have despised a place like this for that very reason. Amazing how circumstances can change your point of view. Now, she felt it was her right to know what people like this stranger were up to.

But he obviously wasn't going to give anything away and was quite plainly delighted to see her cringing with embarrassment.

'Well, if you're ever looking for a place to eat, I own the restaurant across the street. The Feng Shui. We do lunches, dinners and also have a guestroom for rent.' She was gabbling and she knew it.

'Thanks for letting me know,' came the brief reply. 'Goodbye.'

He turned on his heel and made his way down the road towards the harbour.

* * *

Well, how was that for getting the brush-off, she thought angrily as she

14

watched him head towards the end of the street. Then he stopped on the corner and, looking pointedly in her direction, took out a mobile phone.

Drat! If only she'd been a bit cool, and had simply wandered in the same direction as him instead of accosting him, she might have had a chance to hear what he was saying. It was almost as if he was teasing her.

No, she thought, that's just your overactive imagination at work again.

She squared her shoulders and marched back into the restaurant in the same confident manner that she'd marched out of it, just to show him that she was busy with her own stuff and had no interest in him.

'What's he up to then?' Megan's eyes glinted at the sniff of an interesting piece of gossip.

Cassandra sighed and pulled off her jacket, throwing it over the coat-stand. 'I don't know. He wouldn't tell me.'

'Well, you're no use as a private detective!'

'I'm glad you think it's a laugh. You won't when the restaurant gets demolished to make way for a block of flats and you haven't got a job any more. Or worse still, if we get burgled and beaten to a pulp for the day's takings because he *was* casing the joint, after all.'

Cassandra stomped off to the kitchen to prepare the lunch time vegetables in readiness for the arrival of her chef, Jorge, who'd be in later.

Attacking a bunch of innocent carrots, she chopped off their heads with the largest implement she could find — an oversized cleaver — before viciously scraping their skins away with a peeler.

In record time she got through not just the carrots but the onions, the broccoli and the asparagus as well, as angry at herself for being foolish as she was at the stranger for refusing to be drawn by her questions. That was the trouble with men. You could never tell what they were thinking.

As she peeled a pile of potatoes in double-quick time, she thought of

Oliver, and of how she'd thought she'd known what he wanted from life — the same things as her, or so she'd hoped; to settle down and make a life together.

But as it had turned out, what Oliver had been saying and what had been going on in his head were two different things . . .

She took a deep breath. That's what they'd told her to do at relaxation classes, breathe deeply and think good thoughts. Go in your mind to your happy place. *But this is my happy place*, she realised, looking around her bright, quirky little restaurant. *The Feng Shui is my real-life happy place where I've planned to spend the rest of my days. My whole future is here in this lovely historical building in this picturesque old town.*

The Feng Shui restaurant was her haven and she was going to do her best to keep it that way.

Scrubbing her muddy hands at the kitchen sink, she caught sight of herself in the mirror.

Was that woman with the intense, troubled expression really her? Drying her hands, she massaged the lines away from her forehead. She hadn't come to Seaport to allow herself to get wound up by life again. She'd vowed never to let herself get into a state again, and up until now she'd achieved that aim.

Why was it that the stranger in the street had got to her? Was it because he'd made her think of Oliver, with his big silent man act? Well, she could do without men cluttering up her life, she thought, as she heard Jorge call out a greeting to Megan as he arrived for work.

★   ★   ★

After lunch, she had the afternoon to herself before the evening dinner guests arrived and, as the evening approached, she looked out from the sitting-room window of her flat above the restaurant, glancing idly down into the street which had become her home.

London had once been her home and, for a long time, she had loved it for its frenetic action. But it was that action, that relentless grinding activity, that had worn her down in both her personal and her working life and had driven her to seek the solace of a town like Seaport.

She sighed and went through to her bedroom, where she coiled her hair and clipped it on top of her head. Adding a pair of simple earrings, she resisted the temptation to dab scent behind her ears. The last thing her customers wanted was heavy perfume with their dinner. It was one of those tricks of the trade that she had learned and which she strictly adhered to in a bid to increase the success of her small business.

As she walked along the rickety wooden passage past the attic room she had done up ready for paying guests, she felt a warm glow of satisfaction.

The attic room was a gamble. Not everyone wanted to stay near the harbour when there was accommodation available that was closer to the beach, but the builder had done an excellent job, and this was the quiet part of town. She looked in on the room, with its ship-in-a-bottle and its white-painted desk and captain's chair which she had rubbed down herself. All this was hers and no-one could take it away from her.

At least she *hoped* no-one could. She remembered the stranger from earlier that day and immediately found herself worrying about who he could be.

Get to work, she told herself. Get downstairs, take care of your customers and forget all about him.

Downstairs, ever reliable Megan was looking after the first few diners.

'Hi, how's it going?' Cassandra asked her, waving across to Jorge, who was deep in clouds of steam from a bubbling pan.

'Everything's fine. You could have stayed upstairs for a bit longer. We won't get really busy for a while yet.'

But it was better for her to be kept busy, thought Cassandra, as she ran her cloth over the bar.

'Looks like we've got an anniversary couple in tonight.' She nodded at the man and the woman sitting by the window.

'That's right.' Megan looked over at the couple. 'Twenty-five years and still going strong.'

'Offer them each a glass of Cava on the house,' suggested Cassandra.

She stood looking at the middle-aged couple who were holding hands across the table, and sighed. At one time, she'd thought that she and Oliver were about to embark upon a long and happy marriage.

She remembered looking at houses for sale in estate agents' windows, even going secretly to visit one or two of them without him. She'd envisaged him relaxing on a sofa while she made coffee in a smart stainless steel kitchen. But then, her dream had blown up in her face, in a way that she could never have imagined in her worst nightmare.

She tore her gaze away from the

couple who were sharing the sort of easy companionship that would likely never come her way now.

Dragging herself back into the busy present, she went to check that Jorge had everything he needed.

* * *

The evening got even busier. Several couples out for a Friday night treat were there to enjoy the restaurant's trademark French and Oriental fusion dishes, such as rice and soy crab cakes, but there was also a well-behaved table of hen night ladies and a family party who were celebrating a daughter's twenty-first birthday.

Later that evening, during a lull, Megan suggested to Cassandra, 'Why don't you go upstairs and take the weight off your feet for half an hour? I can easily cope on my own for a little while.'

Cassandra rubbed her aching back and decided to take Megan up on her offer. 'OK, if you're sure. I need to make a phone call, anyway.'

Away from the hustle and bustle, she collapsed on her bed in her room. It was the smallest of the two bedrooms and she'd decided not to decorate it for a while as she'd only just finished renovating the spare room with a view to taking in paying guests. But, as she sat on the bed, phone in hand, dialling the number, she noticed a small crack in the corner of the ceiling and decided that she'd better arrange for a builder to look at it pretty soon.

'Hi, Ellie?' she said as the phone was answered at the other end of the line.

'Cassandra! How's business?'

'Great, thanks. Full house tonight and we were busy at lunch time.'

'So, if you've got a full house, there must be some very important reason why you're taking time out to phone me right now.'

'Well, I know I'm probably being stupid, but something happened today that's worrying me and I just wondered if your mum could do me a favour and dig out some information for me.'

'OK, shoot.'

Cassandra told Ellie how worried she was about the stranger who'd been hanging around that morning. Ellie's mother was a leading light of The Seaport Preservation Society and, as such, got to hear about any planning applications as soon as they were put before the local council.

'OK, Cass, I'll ask her. She's staying at my aunt's tonight, but I'll have a word with her when she gets back tomorrow. I haven't heard anything myself and she'll usually have a good old rant and rave if she hears of anyone wanting to spoil Seaport. She's been going on recently about the increase in traffic with all the coach parties that visit nowadays. You sound really worried. Would it help if I came around later for a chat? You could offer me a free coffee.'

Cassandra laughed. 'It's a deal. Especially if you can get your mother on the case. The restaurant should have quietened down nicely by ten-thirty if that's not too late for you?'

'Ten-thirty would be fine. It looks as if it's going to be a nice warm evening. We could take a stroll down to the beach if you fancy some exercise.'

'That sounds a good idea.' Cassandra put down the phone feeling much better having done something practical about her worries.

★ ★ ★

When Ellie arrived, very few customers still lingered, and the two girls sat down to finish off the coffee that was left in the percolator.

'So, who is this mysterious stranger, do you think?'

'You should see him,' piped up Megan, listening in as she poured a liqueur for one of the remaining diners. 'He's a cut above your average Seaport male.'

'That's just one more reason to be

suspicious,' Cassandra stated. 'He has too much of an air of business about him to be just passing through. He's up to something, or after something. He isn't here by chance.'

'Maybe he's thinking of setting up a business here himself. Did you consider that he might actually be a rival restaurateur?'

Cassandra fidgeted with a lock of hair that had come loose from her top-knot.

'That wouldn't worry me much. I can handle a bit of healthy competition. Sometimes it can be a good thing to have two quality restaurants side by side, especially if they're different in character. I doubt if anyone else would come up with the Feng Shui concept around here. So, if he wants to start up a great Italian place or a Spanish tapas bar, I'd be fine with that. But I doubt that's his intention.'

'How can you be so sure?' Ellie finished her coffee.

'Because restaurateurs usually talk to each other. If that was his game, he would have been asking me — even if it was in a round about way — how good business was around here. Whether there was any passing trade, that sort of thing. But he was as closed as a limpet shell.'

Ellie reached for her jacket and passed Cassandra her cream woollen wrap.

'Let's go for that walk. I'm sure you're worrying unnecessarily.'

'Are you OK clearing up, Megan?'

'Yeah, fine. You go and get some fresh air. I'll cash up and Jorge and I'll sort everything for the morning.'

'That girl's worth her weight in truffles,' joked Cassandra.

'Are they more valuable than gold?'

'Probably. We certainly only ever use tiny amounts, but they are lovely, just a tiny bit grated over pasta really sets the tastebuds tingling.'

Rescued!

The two girls strolled through the empty streets and made their way down towards the sea.

'I know you think I'm worrying unnecessarily, Ellie, but I love the tranquil atmosphere of this place. It's really important to me.'

The sea breeze was cool, and Cassandra shivered as she pulled her wrap more closely around herself.

'I know. I understand. Coming here was a new start for you.'

'That's right. And I really needed a new start after . . . well, after everything. I just don't want anything to rock my peaceful little boat.'

They stood looking out across the dark sea, towards Frederickstowe port around the corner. A huge container ship skimmed majestically across the horizon, lumbering its way to China to collect toys or electrical goods, while a smaller ferry trundled into the port bringing visitors from the Hook of Holland across the wide calm expanse of navy blue water. Lights twinkled out of the ship's windows, reflecting in the blackness.

Ellie looked at her friend with sympathy filling her eyes as she said, 'It seems as if very little ever changes here but even Seaport isn't immune to the passage of time. Just take a look down there.'

Cassandra looked in the direction Ellie was pointing, but saw only a grassy bank and a long path running next to it.

'There's nothing much to see.'

'No, there isn't now, but there used to be. Only a few decades back you'd have seen a lovely glass concert hall, like a huge conservatory, where choirs used to sing and bands used to play dance music. It was the hub of the town. You'd never think it to look at it now, would you?'

'No.'

'And you know the two little lighthouses on the beach?'

'Oh, I love those, they're so Victorian.'

'Well, as you know, they're all locked up now, with gates and chains over the stairs, but they weren't always like that. When they were boys, my brother and his friends used to swim out to those lighthouses, climb right to the top and jump off. Everything changes. You can't preserve things for ever.'

Cassandra bit her lip and looked along the beach, adjusting her eyes to the darkness.

'Oh, no,' she breathed.

'What?' Ellie looked around.

'It's him. The snooper from this morning.'

'Where?'

'See, by the old lighthouses. What is he doing prowling around at this time of night?'

'Cass, he's not prowling, he's just walking, like us.'

'That's not all he's doing. See, he's taking photos with a flash. Who on earth takes photos at this time of night?'

'Well, I admit it is a little strange.'

'Of course, if he was thinking of putting up some horrid ugly development along the sea front here, he'd probably want to get rid of the lighthouses. Pull them down. Your mother would fight tooth and nail against that, wouldn't she?'

'She would indeed,' Ellie agreed. 'And not just her. The whole of The Seaport Preservation Society would be right behind her. They'd never let it happen.'

'Even if a stranger came along and offered the council some sort of incentive?' Cassandra said with an edge to her voice. 'There are so many councillors who keep banging on about trying to modernise Seaport. A bit of money goes a long way round here and, from the look of him, I have a horrid feeling our stranger isn't short of ready cash.'

As they stood talking on the beach path, they lowered their voices to a whisper as the stranger passed them by and had the effrontery, as he recognised Cassandra, to raise a sardonic eyebrow and wish her goodnight.

She stared out to sea, mouth tightly shut as if she hadn't heard.

Ellie called a pleasant, 'Goodnight,' and then, once he was safely out of earshot hissed, 'You were very rude not to say anything. And now I know what Megan meant about his looks. Talk about a tall, dark, handsome stranger.'

'Oh, don't you start. Anyway, I wasn't rude. He gave me the silent treatment when I was trying to find out what he was doing here, so now we're quits. Where do you think he's staying?' she asked.

'Well . . . ' Ellie's eyes followed him discreetly as he made his way up the hill. 'I reckon he's probably at the Cliff Hotel, it's the only posh place around here.'

'Good. I know the owner. Perhaps he

can tell me who the guy is.'

'Won't it seem a bit strange, you asking questions about a tall, dark stranger? People will start to think you're a stalker.' Ellie laughed and tugged her friend's arm. 'Come on, Cass, let's get you back; your feet must be killing you after a long day in the restaurant.'

'It's a labour of love,' replied Cassandra. But, walking back up the hill, her feet felt heavier than they'd ever done before.

The only person they passed on their walk was a resident of one of the terraced houses behind Cassandra's restaurant. They nodded goodnight to the lady whose shuffling old Labrador trundled along behind her.

Cassandra often walked these streets alone and never felt threatened by anybody. People here went about their business, passed the time of day with each other, month followed month, and the only thing that changed about the place was the season.

Everything else was familiar and fixed — from the pure blue sea to the sandy beach with its one simple café where you could get tea and cake or a fry-up and not much else.

It was a place where people wanted for nothing and had little to worry about.

Until today, thought Cassandra. And that was her last thought that night as she leaned over to turn off the bedside lamp and listened to the distant sound of the sea as she slowly drifted off to sleep.

★　★　★

The next day was a Saturday, and as they prepared for the lunch time visitors, Megan asked, 'What have you got planned for tomorrow?'

The restaurant didn't open on Sundays, so Cassandra would have the pleasure of a whole day to herself.

'I'm going to a boot fair. I've finally decided to bite the bullet and clear out all that stuff that I've been storing in the summerhouse.'

'What's actually in there? I've never been down the garden. It's a bit too overgrown.'

'I know. Sorting out the garden will be my next big project. Maybe once I've cleared out the summerhouse and I've got the garden straight we can have tables out there. We're getting so popular it would be great if we could fit in more people in the summer,' said Cassandra as she dusted the bottles on the bar. 'Anyway, the summerhouse is crammed with the unwanted bits and bobs left over from my life in London. I thought at one time that I might find a use for some of the stuff here, but it's mostly small pieces of furniture and the trappings of a bachelor girl life in the city. And that's not me at all these days.'

'I think it's always good to get rid of unwanted clutter. It can be hard work, but once you've done it, it's like a weight off your shoulders.'

'Exactly. All the self-help books I've

read have talked about shedding the things you don't use.'

'I guess that Feng Shui stuff is all about that, too.'

'That's right, Megan, you're getting the hang of it. We'd all do well, once in a while, to clear out the corners of our lives where junk collects. My new aim in life is simplicity and a lack of possessions.'

And that includes people who aren't good for me, she thought, as her mind went back to Oliver and the crowd she used to hang out with. When she'd needed help, she'd truly found out who her friends were.

City life had been all about having the best paid job so that you could afford all the latest furniture and gadgets. It had also meant being with people who were endless fun seekers and, if anything happened to you the way it had to Cassandra, they weren't happy to sit in the slow lane while you recovered.

'Are you all right?' asked Megan, 'you

look very far away.'

'I was just thinking,' she said, 'that I haven't missed any of those old possessions. And now I have to watch my pennies, I might just as well sell them. Maybe I'll make enough for new plants for the garden. Selling furniture I don't need and buying some old-fashioned roses and honeysuckle will be more than a fair exchange.'

★ ★ ★

Cassandra set her alarm for five in the morning, happy to get up with the seagulls who whirled around in the sky, seeming to cheer her on as she loaded the contents of the old summerhouse into her car.

Hard physical work was the perfect way to forget all her concerns about the stranger, she thought, as she piled two smart chrome lampstands and a nest of glass coffee tables into the car. A DVD player and the smart portable television she had kept in her modern London flat

37

were the next things to be loaded in.

She smiled and shook her head. When did she ever get the chance to watch television nowadays? Anyway, it was far nicer to be either in the restaurant or walking on the beach, watching the real world go by rather than some pretend TV world.

Then she opened the drawers of a smart, mirrored, bedside chest and inside, face down, were a pile of photos in frames. With a jolt, she remembered hiding away the photos of herself and Oliver and all her so-called 'friends' from her old life. She hadn't had the heart to throw them out at the time, but at last she felt she might be strong enough to do so. She ran her hand across one of the photos. She'd looked so happy back then, but it had all turned out so badly. So many memories, so far away in time and space.

Occasionally, her old life would come back to haunt her like this but she resolved not to dwell upon it.

She would remove the photos from

the frames when she got to the boot fair, and at least the frames themselves should make a pound or two.

Also in the drawers were other mementoes that she'd buried so thoroughly that she'd barely thought about them in over a year — a musical box which played *On The Isle Of Capri*, bought when Oliver had whisked her there for a weekend, and a shell necklace he had bought for her in California.

Her life back then had seemed so glamorous.

She shoved the shell necklace, the photos and the box back into the bedside cabinet and heaved it into the car. The sooner she sold all this stuff, the better.

As she was examining a pair of smart white curtains which had been fine in her high-rise flat, but which were much too long for any of the windows in her restaurant, she heard a scuffle and a miaow. Looking down, she saw a pair of bright green eyes peering out at her from amongst the jumble. Then a small, skinny, grey kitten emerged, looking nervous but pleased to see someone.

'Hello, Kitty.' Cassandra held out her hand and the little cat rubbed his face along her arm. One of the few things she'd never been able to have when she'd been in London was a pet, because it wasn't fair to keep an animal in a penthouse flat, especially if you were out all day.

Besides, Oliver hadn't liked cats.

The cat looked at her quizzically and began to purr.

'Are you a stray? Well, I'm sorry, but I don't have time to fuss you right now. I can get you some scraps from the kitchen, though.'

She picked up the kitten and noted how bony he felt beneath his grey fur. He must have been existing on fish scraps thrown out of the fishermens' nets.

'You've been living in my summer-house for a while, haven't you?'

When she returned from the kitchen

with a saucerful of chicken scraps, the kitten took no time gobbling them up. Then he sat washing his whiskers as she finished tidying the summer-house.

* * *

Cassandra's back ached with all the lifting and from the effort of squeezing everything into the car, but finally it was done and it was still only seven-thirty in the morning.

The boot fair was being held some distance from the coast, in a field owned by the local county rugby club.

As she said goodbye to the little cat, who she'd christened Smokey, she stroked his head and said, 'That's two good things that have happened to me today. Not only am I finally getting rid of the remnants of my old life, but I've also met you and, hopefully, if you like it here, you'll stay.'

He let out a chirrup of a miaow, and Cassandra carefully pulled shut the gate, hoping she would find him there when she returned.

★   ★   ★

The rugby club field was a good half-hour's drive from Seaport, along narrow, winding country roads. As she drove, Cassandra looked out at the fields planted with corn and barley that were spread out on either side of her. How could I ever have endured the concrete grey of city life, she wondered.

Looking at the dashboard clock, she was pleased to see that she was in good time for the fair. Although it was hardly a relaxing way to spend one of her precious few days off, she felt sure it would be worth all the effort in the end. There was something very cleansing about shrugging off a life which didn't fit you any more.

Then, suddenly, driving around a corner on the narrow road, she had to brake hard to avoid hitting a fox, and stalled the car. When she tried to restart the engine, nothing happened. She tried again, but still to no avail.

Oh dear! She didn't pretend to know anything about cars, but she might as well get out and have a look. And as soon as she opened the driver's door, she saw on the road, on the right hand side by the front bumper, a big puddle of black oil.

Starting to feel agitated, her hands sweating, she got back into the car to pull the lever that would spring open the bonnet. She thought she'd better take a look at the engine although what she knew about cars could be written on a grain of rice. But she knew enough to realise — as she lifted the bonnet and peered underneath — that car engines weren't meant to be liberally spattered with oil.

There was nothing she could do about this herself. She'd just have to wait for someone to come along so she could beg a lift either home or to the nearest garage.

My, this was dismal, she thought, looking at the car bursting at the seams with all her stuff. If she didn't get to the boot fair today, she'd have to take the whole lot home again and stash it back in the summerhouse.

Suddenly, she heard a car approaching and she stood out in the road, hoping that the driver would stop. Amazingly, the young couple in the car didn't seem to notice that she was needing assistance and drove straight past.

Her heart fell into her boots.

Then a sporty, blue MG appeared over the rise in the road and she walked out into the middle of the tarmac, jumping up and down and waving frantically.

As the MG drew closer, she was overjoyed to see the car slowing down.

But her joy turned to horror as she recognised the driver. Of all the people to have to ask for help! It was the tall dark stranger who'd worried her so much the day before. This was not her lucky day. She gritted her teeth as the car pulled up and the man unfolded his long legs to get out.

'You look as if you've got a problem.'

'I'm afraid I have.'

He'd ditched the hand-tailored suit today and was wearing jeans and a black sweatshirt. Far more suitable for fiddling with cars, she couldn't help thinking.

She also couldn't help thinking that Megan had been right. He *was* seriously good-looking.

Well, as they say, any port in a storm and she was definitely adrift in a storm, so she raised a smile and said, 'I can't get it to go into gear and I'm leaking oil.'

The stranger peered under the bonnet and Cassandra peered too, feeling quite useless. The scent of his newly-washed hair and lemony after-shave drifted towards her on the early morning air.

She doubted whether he knew much about cars either; he looked far too superior to be the sort to get his hands dirty.

'Hmm. It's hard to tell whether it's engine oil or transmission oil. Have you checked your oil levels?'

'I haven't. I've only just stopped, but I'll go and get a rag from the boot and do it now.'

She fetched a rag and went back round to the front of the car. Hoping she didn't look totally clueless, she pulled out the engine dipstick and peered at it.

He studied her as she studied it and she wondered desperately what he was thinking.

He looked slightly amused, as if he knew she was trying to make a good impression.

'What do you think?' he asked.

'I think the engine oil's fine. It must be something else.'

Now she was stumped as she'd reached the limits of her mechanical knowledge.

'Mmm. Yes, it looks like a problem

with your automatic transmission oil.'

He reached inside the engine and pulled out an orange plastic plug with a long wire on the end and said, 'That's your problem. See? It's as dry as a bone. You're lucky you haven't ruined your gearbox altogether. There's no chance you'll get any further, though. You need to get a garage to look at this car. I think they might have to strip the gearbox.'

That sounded incredibly expensive. Cassandra gulped and let out a sigh which she would rather have kept from him.

This was a disaster.

She'd hoped to have a day out and make a little money, and now here she was stranded and looking at a possible bill of hundreds of pounds.

'Oh dear, I could really do without this.'

She thought she saw a look of sympathy cross his face, but it wasn't his problem. The most help she could expect from him was an offer to stop at a garage if he passed one and to ask them to come and tow her car away.

'Well,' he said, rolling up his sleeves to reveal strong tanned forearms, 'I suppose I could take a look.'

'Oh, would you?'

'I used to be into cars when I was a teenager.'

With that, he got down on his knees on the road.

'Wait,' she said, 'I've got some bubblewrap in the boot.' She took the sheet of plastic that had been folded around the coffee tables and positioned it so that he could lie on it underneath the car.

⋆   ⋆   ⋆

She waited with baited breath, hoping that there was some way he could help. It would be a nightmare if she had to have the car towed home.

'Can you see what the problem is?' she called to him.

'I can.' He slid out, hands filthy with

oil. 'For some reason, the pipe has come loose. I might have something in my toolkit which will solve the problem.'

He went back to his sports car and rummaged around in a toolbox.

'Good. This jubilee clip should do the job.'

After a bit more tinkering under her car, he emerged again.

'There, that'll hold it nicely. The only thing you need now is some new oil. There's a garage not far from here. I know because I passed it a while back. Would you like to come with me to get the oil, or will you wait with the car? This is a lonely road, so I'd rather you didn't wait on your own.'

'If you don't mind I *will* come. Here, your hands are filthy. I've got some wipes in my car.'

Her sense of relief at his help was enormous. Maybe he wasn't quite so bad after all?

'Now I'm clean enough to introduce

myself properly,' he said holding out a hand. 'Adam Hawthorne.'

'I'm Cassandra Waverley. And thank you, thank you so much for stopping to help me.'

A Threat To Seaport?

They got into his MG and drove off down the winding lane. It was a seriously impractical car, only two seats and little room for luggage, unlike her sturdy Vauxhall Astra. Fast cars usually equalled a fast lifestyle, she thought, studying him out of the corner of her eye. She'd known men like him in London. They flitted in and out of women's lives like they flitted in and out of trendy bars, only thinking of today and only living in the present.

As they breezed along the country lanes in the early sunshine with the full-leafed trees arching above them like a tunnel, Cassandra could contain her curiosity no longer.

'So, what brings you to Seaport, Mr Hawthorne? I'm sure you're not here just to prowl the streets taking photographs, or to help women in distress.'

'No, I wish my job was as easy as that. And please, call me Adam. Well, Cassandra, I run a location finding agency — We look out for film locations on behalf of movie and TV companies, and I'm here sussing out the possibilities of Seaport on behalf of a client.'

Cassandra was puzzled.

'Oh. Right. Is it a nature programme that your client's thinking of filming here? There are some wonderful waders and other birds on the mud flats past the beach huts.'

'No.' He shook his head. 'Nothing as peaceful as a nature programme, I'm afraid.'

Cassandra could feel herself tensing. 'Well, peacefulness is the very essence of this area, Mr Hawthorne — sorry, I mean, Adam. Apart from being well-known to those tourists who come here year after year because they value its tranquillity, Seaport is a bit of a hidden treasure.'

'Oh, it's a treasure all right, precisely because there hasn't been a huge amount of development.'

The high verges on either side of them were scattered with bright red poppies, which nodded and bowed and then stood to attention again as the MG sped past.

'It's the fact that the town is unspoilt that make it the ideal setting for my client's project.'

'Which is?'

'A television drama about the life of Pepys.'

'A drama? A series, you mean?'

'That's right. I'm sure you know Samuel Pepys was a local MP.'

'I do. Seaport has a very rich past; it's one of the reasons I chose to live here.'

'Well, I think a lot more people will become interested in the area if the series gets the go ahead.'

That's what I'm afraid of, thought Cassandra.

'It'll be a minor series though, won't it? Not something of interest to the mass market?' She knew she was clutching at straws, willing it to be so.

'Oh no. It's to be a big budget production. The series would be screened overseas as well as in the UK. It's a well-known production company that's asked me to look at the possibilities of filming around here. They've bought the film rights to a recent, best-selling biography about Pepys and the only thing that remains now is to decide when to film it and where. From what I've seen of it so far, Seaport looks ideal.'

Yes, Seaport was ideal, thought Cassandra.

Ideal for people wanting to get away from hassle.

Ideal for people who wanted to live a quiet life.

'You know, I don't think I like the sound of this. Seaport has its own very individual personality and places can be destroyed so easily if the outside world swarms in.'

'Swarms in? You make the prospect of outsiders sound like an invasion of killer bees. The series could be filmed elsewhere, of course. We can create practically any sort of setting, any-where.'

'You can?' She could feel the tension slipping away slightly. If they could recreate her beloved town on a set somewhere far away, then it wouldn't be invaded and disrupted.

'Oh, yes. I've been asked in the past to find a snow-covered mountainside that was needed for a stills shoot for a car advert, the only trouble being that the budget was too small to go outside the UK and the advertising company were doing the shoot in mid-summer. So I sent one of my location managers to do a recce in Wales. We had to look for somewhere that wasn't on a busy road as we had to stop the traffic while the stills were being taken, but once we'd found such a place it was just a case of spraying foam in the back-ground and unloading tons of salt in the foreground. By the time we'd finished it looked just like Switzerland in the middle of winter.'

He sounded very pleased with

himself but, all the while, Cassandra was boiling-up with rage.

'And what about the local people who lived there? How much fun did they have seeing everything turned upside down like that?'

'Oh, we always have to sweet-talk the locals. That's part of my job, to smooth over troubled waters with the local council, the police, maybe a local farmer who owns the land we want to use.'

'That sounds like a huge amount of disruption for one photograph. How much of an upset would filming a major TV series cause?'

'It's true that there'll be huge quantities of gear and trailers involved; after all, the crew need to fed and watered.'

'So they don't even use the local facilities? They just bowl in, bring their own food and drink, create chaos and clear off again?'

'I wouldn't put it quite like that.'

'No, I'm sure you wouldn't but, don't

you see, a small place like Seaport couldn't cope with such disruption and remain unchanged? And it's not even as if the town's small businesses would benefit from any extra trade — not if the film company is so self-contained.'

Luckily, they'd just arrived at the garage so they were distracted from a full-blown argument.

Cassandra could see that Adam was put out by her outburst, probably thinking that he was getting poor thanks for helping her out. But she'd always been a woman who said what she thought.

* * *

At the garage, Adam took charge and decided on the brand of oil her car needed, which was a good thing as Cassandra was too preoccupied with what he'd been telling her to think straight about such practicalities.

The prospect of a film crew invading her carefully chosen patch of peace and quiet filled her with horror. And worse, what would happen afterwards? If the film was a huge success and raised Seaport's profile, they'd be invaded yet again, probably by coaches full of day-trippers squeezing through the narrow streets and turning an historically pretty area into a media-inspired circus.

★ ★ ★

It didn't take long to get back to her car. Deftly, Adam tipped first one litre of oil, then a second into the engine and she was delighted to see, when she turned the key in the ignition, that the warning light had gone off.

When she heard the automatic transmission click into gear she knew he had worked magic and she would make it to her boot sale after all.

'So, where were are you off to with all this stuff?' he asked her.

'I'm on my way to a boot sale. There's one held every month in a field not far from here that's owned by the local rugby club. I thought I could offload some junk, make a few pounds and have a day out in the fresh air into the bargain. It's quite pretty countryside round about. Not the sort of thing you'd be interested in at all.'

'I *am* interested actually. I'm taking photographs of a variety of possible locations, so a field that's available for rent and that's surrounded by pretty countryside could well be worth a look. Besides, I suspect you could do with some help getting that lot out of your car at the other end.'

Cassandra looked at the small items of furniture and bits and pieces which had taken her so long to load up. The last thing she wanted was to provide Adam with possible locations but then . . .

'It's very kind of you to offer, but I won't put you to any more trouble. If you'd like to follow me in your car, though, I can show you the way to the field where the boot sale is being held, and you could soon see if the location is of interest to you.'

They made their way through the next village and soon arrived at the site of the boot sale, where all the cars were being directed into lines and the stallholders were already busy polishing and pricing their wares.

Adam went away to park in the visitors' area but soon reappeared.

'I haven't been to a boot sale since I was in my teens,' he said. 'My parents would go to one every now and then and I remember selling off all my old books and records. I used to quite enjoy the bargaining.'

'That's something I'm absolutely no good at,' she admitted, lugging a box of books out of the car.

Without her asking, Adam unloaded the television, the nest of tables and the mirrored bedroom chest, leaving her to deal with the lighter things like the lamps and the DVD player, and she soon had a very respectable display of goods, ready for when the buyers arrived.

The sun was beginning to warm up and Adam stripped off his sweatshirt to reveal a short-sleeved black T-shirt. It was obvious from his physique that he was no stranger to the gym.

'Thank you for helping. I really didn't want to put you to any more trouble. But, as I was a bit late getting here, I have to say it's been a real bonus having someone else around,' Cassandra told him gratefully.

'I've enjoyed it,' said Adam and then, at her look of disbelief he insisted, 'Honestly, I really have. It's good to get out and get a bit of exercise. Over the past few days, I've done nothing more energetic than take photographs and write up my reports.'

'Well, thank you, anyway. There's a tent over there where they sell coffee. Could I buy you a cup?'

'Great, I'll have a cappuccino, thanks.' Cassandra couldn't help laughing as he spread his hands and said, 'What's up, did I say something funny?'

'Well, you sound just like I did when

I first came here from London. I think the choice as far as coffee is concerned will be instant with or without. And that's with or without milk or sugar. We don't get much more fancy than that around here.'

'Ok, then mine's instant with milk and without sugar, thanks.'

* * *

She also brought back a couple of slices of home-made lemon drizzle cake. 'I happen to know you can't get anything as good as this in the coffee shops in London.'

'Mmm, you're right. This is superb.'

They sat on two fold-up garden chairs that she'd brought along to sell and, after licking his fingers and downing his coffee in one, Adam asked, 'So what are you doing down here if you've lived in London? All this furniture's top-notch stuff, the sort you'd see in one of those trendy loft conversions. You must have been doing pretty well for yourself.'

'I was, in a way.' A sadness crept into her voice and a cloud came over her normally bright features. 'I was what they call a structurer, working in a bank.'

'Wow! That's working in high finance! That's a pretty specialised job isn't it?'

'It is. It's also very stressful.'

She twirled a strand of hair around her fingers. Just the thought of her previous way of life set off the old feelings of tightness in her chest.

'It's a job that involves twelve-hour days; endless presentations to the dealers; piles of responsibility; deadlines.'

There was concern in Adam's eyes as he studied her. 'I've heard that the banks certainly get their pound of flesh from their structurers, even though the returns are good.'

'Oh, yes, the wages are fabulous, more than I'd ever dreamed of earning. But the thing is, the banks buy you. They virtually own you. They want every second of your time. You're almost chained to your desk.'

'That bad, huh?'

'Well, when I started in the job, they sent me off to New York for six weeks to train. They put me up in a top class hotel right near the office, and they sent a car to fetch me every day.'

'Sounds wonderful.'

'Yes, it *sounds* wonderful. But what I didn't realise back then was that they wanted to make sure I spent every waking moment working for them. When I got back to London, I thought the pressure would ease off a bit. All my friends from university had normal jobs and went out and had fun in the evenings, but my job wasn't like that.'

'What *was* it like?'

'It seemed like luxury, to begin with. The office building was amazing. There was a gym on site, and there were even food outlets within the building; well-known coffee shops and pizza parlours. But the place was designed so they could keep you there all day. You had no need to go out, so you simply lived, ate and breathed work all the time.'

'That sounds intense.'

She looked away into the distance, not wanting to remember. Most of all, not wanting to remember Oliver, who was part of that past life and who had, in the end, treated her so badly.

'It was awful, although it took me quite a while to realise it. That's why I'm so pleased to be getting rid of all this stuff. It reminds me of a way of life that nearly destroyed me.'

She suddenly clammed up and turned away from him. She didn't want to have to explain herself to a stranger and, seeing a potential customer advancing towards her stall, she stood up.

'How much for this nest of glass tables?' the man asked.

Cassandra named a figure, deliberately pitching it low, keen to make her first sale.

The customer started to reach into his pocket.

'Actually,' said Adam, 'I'm afraid they'll cost you more than that. Sorry,

Cassandra, I forgot to tell you — there's a chap coming back in a minute who's very keen and he's offered me double that amount for those tables.'

She stood with her mouth open. She didn't know what he was talking about. They hadn't spoken to any customers yet!

'OK then,' said the man, rapidly pulling out a bundle of notes. 'I'll match his price. It's over the top but I like the items.'

He walked off with the small tables.

'What was all that about?' asked Cassandra, amazed.

'When you were away getting the coffee,' said Adam. 'I wandered around a few of the other stalls and chatted to some of the regulars. That man's a dealer, so is that one over there, *and* that guy in the distance, the one in the brown jacket. As it is, he'll make twice what he paid you for those tables when he sells them on, but he'd have been happy to fleece you and give you a fraction of what they were worth.'

Cassandra was beginning to see Adam in a new light.

'Thank you. All I wanted was to get rid of them.'

'That's what those guys count on. They're not interested in paying an honest price or playing fair. Believe me, I've encountered their sort in the past.'

'You have?'

He stood, his hands in his pockets, looking into the distance before he turned his gaze back towards her. For the first time she noticed how dark his eyes were, except for the little gold flecks that gave them depth and sensitivity.

'I used to be a policeman. It was a long time ago. But when I was in the force, as you can imagine, I met all sorts of people. Good people, bad people. Rogues and ruffians, saints and people just trying to get along. It's a job that teaches you a lot about human nature.'

'Although it could make a person too hard-bitten, and somewhat jaded about their fellow man?' suggested Cassandra.

'You get over it.' He smiled as if to prove that under that hard exterior there was a sense of humour.

A small gaggle of customers suddenly gathered around the stall, asking questions and bargaining, and Cassandra and Adam had soon sold the television and the DVD player.

The sudden flurry of activity was replaced by another lull.

She took the opportunity to ask, 'So, how did a former policeman come to be running a film location company?'

'Pure chance,' he explained to her. 'I'd tried my hand at various jobs. At one point, I thought I might as well set up a private security firm, like lots of ex-policemen do. But I wanted to get away from all that. In my spare time, I'd always been a keen photographer, and one day I saw an advert in the paper, looking for people who enjoyed photography and were free to travel. I had to take care of a few personal things first, but I was largely free, since I'd no dependants any more.' He swallowed. 'I'm a widower,' he explained, and his face came under such a cloud that Cassandra could have kicked herself for asking him questions about himself.

'I . . . I'm sorry. Forgive me, I didn't mean to intrude.'

'It's a while ago now. I'm over the worst.'

Cassandra wasn't too sure about that but felt an urgent need to steer him away from a difficult subject.

'You were telling me about your work.'

'That's right. Well, the advert turned out to be for a Location Manager which, as I've explained, is someone who finds good spots to film or photograph TV ads, programmes and movies.'

'Well, it all sounds very glamorous!'

'Actually, we find most of our locations within the area inside the M25! But the TV series which might be shot in Seaport is a big deal for us, if we can secure it.'

Cassandra looked away, she didn't even want to think about that.

She pounced on a possible customer, simply not wanting to talk to Adam about his current project.

The customer was interested in the chest of drawers and had begun opening them before she remembered about the photographs in their frames. She hastily removed them, putting them aside, but after she'd sold the chest, she saw, that Adam was studying the photos of her old friends and Oliver, and quickly took them from him, placing them face down in the back of the car.

'Sorry,' he said, 'did I do something wrong?'

She shrugged. 'I should have got rid of those photos ages ago. It's not good to hang on to things that are no longer of any use.'

His eyebrows knitted with concern but she could see his old policeman ways hadn't left him. He was curious by nature.

'It looks like you had a lot of good

friends — you look happy in those pictures. Any half-decent photographer can tell when people are posing or not and you seemed to be having a whale of a time. Why did you leave London and all those good friends behind?'

She held up her chin and tried to sound breezy instead of upset at selling off what were once prized possessions. 'I've moved on from all that. I'm like a snake sloughing off its old skin.'

'More like a caterpillar emerging as a butterfly, I would say.'

Cassandra blushed. It was such a long time since anyone had flirted with her!

She turned towards the next potential customer, warning herself that Adam Hawthorne was a charmer who probably had an ulterior motive for aiming his sweet-talk in her direction.

Beware of wolves in sheep's clothing her mother had always said. The only thing was, this wolf could prove mighty difficult to resist.

* * *

By lunch time, they had sold everything and Cassandra felt a hundred times better than she had at the beginning of the day.

As they got ready to go, she turned to Adam and said, 'I'm so grateful for all your help today. If it hadn't been for you, I'd still be at the side of the road with a broken-down car full of unwanted junk. Instead, I've had a really enjoyable and successful day. So, please, if you fancy a really good meal on the house tomorrow, I'd be very happy to see you at my restaurant.'

'Only if you're willing to have dinner *with* me rather than waiting on me.'

She was taken aback. Her cheeks turned a hot pink. She hadn't meant that at all, but after the help he'd given her it would be churlish to turn him down.

'I'm sure I can spare a little time to sit and eat with you, but on one condition.'

'What's that?' The corners of his mouth began to turn up in a smile.

'That you let me attempt to persuade

you that Seaport is definitely not the film location that your clients are looking for.'

'Well, they say there's no such thing as a free lunch and I guess that applies to dinners as well. Let's say seven o'clock, shall we?'

They parted on good terms and, as Cassandra drove back through the bright sunshine, she decided that the warm glow she felt inside was down to her bulging purse full of notes. After all, it couldn't possibly have anything to do with Adam Hawthorne.

★　★　★

She spent that Sunday afternoon in the garden, determined to make a start on her project of making it fit for customers' use. She searched everywhere for the little cat but, in the way cats do, it had gone off somewhere else.

Suddenly, without it, without anyone, she felt lonely. The restaurant was closed and, although this place was her piece of heaven, at the moment it seemed like rather an empty one.

But she resolved not to brood and put on a pair of old jeans and a T-shirt, tied back her hair, took a cup of coffee out into the garden and started to weed.

The physical work improved her spirits no end, and while she weeded and dug over the old flower beds, her mind drifted to Adam Hawthorne and the sad look that had come into his eyes when he'd spoken of his wife.

★   ★   ★

After she'd finished for the day, she collapsed in an easy chair in her sitting-room in her flat above the restaurant. In front of her on the coffee table was a plan she'd drawn of the garden showing a small bower, a little raised pond, and room for four tables and chairs where she could seat at least another twenty guests.

If she could make enough money over the next few years, she could afford to build a conservatory extension which would increase her winter takings as well as her summer ones. She smiled. Making plans to expand her little restaurant fulfilled her in a way that no other activity did.

It was while she was thinking all this through that the doorbell rang, and she went down to find that it was Ellie who stood on the doorstep, chirpy as ever.

'Hi, Cass, how are you? Can I come in for a minute?'

'Sure, I was just sitting down to tea and cake. Want some?'

'Mmm, that sounds great. Guess what?'

Cassandra could see Ellie was bursting with news.

'What?'

'Mum's back and she's been doing a bit of digging around about your stranger. He's some sort of film production guy; they're wanting to make a TV series here, isn't it exciting?'

Cassandra poured the tea and cut them each a piece of chocolate cake.

'Actually, I've managed to find out

that much by myself.' And she related to an open-mouthed Ellie the events of the morning.

'Wow! So he doesn't sound so bad after all.'

'Just because he was helpful, doesn't mean that I'm happy with what he's doing. Don't you see what this might mean, Ellie?'

'Well, I don't really see a problem.'

'That's because you don't run a business here. If these film people come here, they'll totally disrupt the whole town. And they won't even contribute anything to the local economy because they'd bring all their own catering with them. They wouldn't, for example, use a restaurant like this. And they'd have massive great trucks and trailers blocking up the streets so that the customers who do want to come here would find it difficult to park.

'Then, once the series has been made, if it's a big success, we'd become some sort of horrid version of an English Disneyland. There'll be tacky

Pepys souvenir shops all over the place selling mugs and key chains and T-shirts. This lovely, unspoiled old town will become like any other commercialised stop-off for day-trippers. It'll lose all its character and you won't be able to move for people. Is that really what you want for your home town?'

Cassandra was sad when she saw the excitement drain away from Ellie's face, but it was the truth.

'Oh, when you put it like that I suppose it doesn't sound so good. I was looking forward to seeing a few TV stars that's all. I didn't think about what would happen to the town. But wouldn't the nature of any knock-on effects depend on what sort of series they're planning to film?'

'I guess so. If it's very commercialised, I think my nightmare scenario will come true. If it's a quieter, classier series things might be different. But I'm resolved to do anything I can to stop them filming here.'

'Well, anyway,' said Ellie, 'Mum

asked me to pass on the news that The Seaport Preservation Society has got wind of the plans for this TV series and they're holding a public meeting tomorrow morning if you want to go to it. Also, I've to warn you that one of the Society's members, Councillor Watson, is apparently all for the filming to go ahead.'

'Oh, him! Yes, I can imagine Bill Watson would be keen to put Seaport in the public eye.'

'You know him, then?'

'I certainly do. I also happen to know that one of his golfing buddies is the property developer who's bought the old warehouse on the other side of the harbour, and that he's applied for planning permission to convert the building into a complex of small shops. I'm sure the two of them stand to make a packet out of any publicity, good or otherwise. They're the sort who'd be only too happy to see more cheap gift shops and tacky souvenir outlets springing up in the town. The old book shops and the tasteful antique outlets will be replaced with shops selling badly made pirate suits and plastic replicas of boats. It'll be ghastly, it really will.'

Cassandra could feel the skin on the back of her neck prickling, a sure sign that she was getting overwrought. She rubbed the tense muscles which were stiffening and threatening to leave her with a headache.

Ellie placed a comforting hand on her shoulder. 'This is really getting to you, isn't it?'

'It's come at the worst time! I've got the business going really well and now I've got great plans for the garden.'

Ellie got up to leave. 'I have to go now, but I'll be at the meeting tomorrow. We'll all have a chance to object then. If you put your point as forcefully there as you have to me, I'm sure a lot of people will be on your side. See you tomorrow, and try not to worry too much.'

A Threat To Cassie?

The meeting hall was more crowded than Cassandra had ever seen it.

Every seat was filled and there were crowds of people standing at the back of the tiny hall. She squeezed her way through and found the seat which Ellie had been saving for her.

'This is extraordinary! I've never seen so many people here. I didn't know The Seaport Preservation Society had so many members.' Ellie had to raise her voice to be heard over the chatter of all the people.

'News has travelled fast. I never knew so many people cared about Seaport. Look, even my neighbour, Jasper Eames, has crawled out from under his piles of old books,' Cassandra declared, giving Jasper a wave which he eagerly returned. 'Looks like I'm not the only one with concerns.' She felt suddenly buoyed up, hoping that the hall was full of objectors and not people who thought the TV series would be a good idea.

★   ★   ★

At that point, Lester Wade, chairman of the society, called the meeting to order with difficulty.

'I think you all know why we're here. Rumours have been going around the town that a TV film is to be made in the area and I know that there are differing views on this; some of us see it as an opportunity to publicise the attractions of Seaport, others view it as a threat to our quiet way of life. But however we feel, we may be powerless to stop it.'

Cassandra felt her heart sink at his words.

He went on, 'Before they can go ahead with the production, the film company will need to seek permission to do so from the local authorities and the police. But if the authorities can't find any reason to object to the film being made in and around the town, then the film crew may be here within a few weeks.'

Then Councillor Bill Watson, a red-faced, corpulent man, rose to his feet.

'I cannot emphasise stronly enough what a great opportunity this could be for our town. We have been trying for years to have Seaport put on the map and now it could finally happen,' he declared.

A few shouts of, 'Hear, hear,' were heard from his council cronies, and Cassandra recognised amongst them Councillor Watson's golfing buddy — the one who'd been buying up land for shopping developments.

Ellie's mother raised her hand. 'As a long term member of a society that exists to preserve the essential character of Seaport, I'm afraid I must object to the filming. I think it would be very naïve of us all to welcome this proposal with open arms.

'We have to think very clearly about how we want Seaport to be perceived by the outside world, and I believe that a TV series will put a plastic gloss on the true historical nature of our town. We also need to remember that the resulting publicity is liable to put pressure on the town's road system and disrupt the tranquillity of our streets.'

As the meeting went on it became clear that people's views were very much polarised. They were either greatly in favour or definitely against the TV series being filmed in their town.

Then Cassandra was nudged by Ellie to look over towards the corner of the room. There, standing in a doorway, trying to look insignificant and not saying a word, was Adam Hawthorne.

Cassandra's heart missed a beat.

Why she should experience that reaction on spotting him, she didn't know, although he certainly looked very dashing; the perfect gentleman in a loosely-tailored black suit and tie.

She didn't know how long he'd been there; had he arrived well before the meeting started in order to circulate around the hall, spreading his views and trying to get the townsfolk on his side beforehand? Suddenly all she could think of was that he reminded her of a spider sitting in the centre of a web, waiting to grab at what he wanted.

Anger began to rise in her, although she knew that he had as much right as anyone to be present at what was a public meeting. But as tempers began to fray and the discussion became more heated, one thing was for certain — Cassandra blamed all this disharmony and sniping on Adam Hawthorne and his unwelcome presence in her once peaceful town.

Finally, unable to hold her peace any longer, she stood up and strongly voiced her opinions against the possible filming.

'I am hoping to expand my business but I want to do it in the lovely town I thought Seaport was, not in the over-crowded manic town Seaport might become if this goes ahead.'

'Then you ought to think very carefully about what's really good for Seaport as a whole, not just for yourself,' snapped Councillor Watson, jabbing his finger in the air. 'Remember, too, that you'll have to seek planning permission for any extension to your restaurant. It's likely to be a lot easier for people like you to get permission, young lady, if the town is geared up for an influx of tourists. It's no use trying to wrap Seaport in cotton wool. That's the sort of thing incomers are prone to do. Remember, an inability to embrace new things is bad for business and will be bad for our town.'

As he spoke, a photographer from the local paper flashed his camera, catching Councillor Watson red-faced and passionate. It would make a superb front page story, thought Cassandra, stinging from his attack.

★   ★   ★

As the meeting broke up and people moved, chattering and arguing, out into the street, she felt completely crestfallen. Councillor Watson's threat had been perfectly obvious to her — if she continued to voice objections, he might make it difficult for her to get planning permission from the council to build a conservatory on to the back of her restaurant.

Suddenly, her arm was caught in a firm grip.

'I'm sorry about that.' Adam Hawthorne's dark eyes were looking down at her. 'Councillor Watson was out of order.'

'If you hadn't come here stirring things up none of this would have happened.' Cassandra shook herself free and walked off.

★　★　★

She was back in the restaurant in time to help with the lunch time service, but she found it very difficult to keep her mind on her work, and it showed.

First she picked up a couple of plates and clumsily dropped one, sending it crashing to the floor to smash into smithereens. Then, when she was helping Jorge prepare a fruit salad, a washed bowl of grapes slid out of her hands, and the grapes tumbled across the kitchen floor in all directions.

Two seconds later, Megan, hurrying out of the kitchen on her way to take an order, let out a wail as she slipped on one of the grapes and fell, cracking her elbow on the side of some shelves.

'Oh, Megan,' cried Cassandra as she rushed to the girl's side. 'Are you OK?'

'Ouch! I'm not sure. My arm! It's agony.'

Cassandra said, 'I'm so sorry. Oh, it's all my fault. Do you think your arm's broken?'

'I don't know.' Megan's face was contorted with agony.

Cassandra phoned the doctor who said he'd call round as soon as he could.

He arrived half an hour later and examined the waitress's swollen and bruised arm in the comfort of Cassandra's upstairs lounge.

'It's not broken, it's just a bad sprain,' he told the two girls, 'but I shall have to strap it up and put your arm in a sling. There'll be no more serving lunches for you for a while young lady. I can give you a lift back home if that would be helpful?'

'It would be very helpful, thank you, doctor,' Cassandra replied on Megan's behalf. The girl was so willing, Cassandra could see she was about to protest that she didn't need to go back home.

After she'd shown Megan and the doctor out, she shut the door and breathed in long and hard as she leaned against it. How was she going to cope without Megan to help her?

*   *   *

Once lunches were over and she'd waved goodbye to Jorge, she went out to sit on the back step in the relative calm of the garden. She bit her lip and felt her eyes beginning to fill with tears. Then, out of the undergrowth, she heard a tiny, plaintive miaow. Padding nervously towards her was Smokey. She swept the tiny cat up into her arms and buried her face in his warm bony body, listening to him purr.

'At least we have each other, eh, Smokey?'

★   ★   ★

Cassandra found some fish bits in the fridge and put down a bowlful of them in front of the cat. His tiny, skinny body hunched over the bowl as his little pink tongue darted in and out. He was starving, poor thing. She watched as he ate greedily, shaking his head as he gulped down the scraps.

Leaning against a kitchen cupboard, she hugged herself, agonising over the events of the past few days. Everything had seemed to be going so well for her.

Until, that is, Adam Hawthorne had crashed into her life, turning all her carefully made plans upside down.

She threw back her head as if looking to heaven — how could she have been so utterly, pathetically helpless as to have needed his help with her car and at the boot fair?

And now Megan, her rock, had been laid up. What on earth was she going to do? She found her breathing becoming shallow and it felt as if she couldn't fill her lungs. Oh no, it couldn't be happening again. She must control it, she must take herself in hand. Cassandra stumbled to the sink, grabbed a glass, filled it with water and gulped it down.

She knew what this feeling meant. She filled the glass again, her hand beginning to shake as she walked purposefully back out into her newly cleared garden. Sit, she told herself. Sit here on this step and breathe deeply, one, two, three. She'd had panic attacks before, only twice, thank goodness, but both times this was how they'd started.

As she sat quietly on her garden step, her mind went back to the first awful time it had happened.

★ ★ ★

She and Oliver had arranged to go out to dinner. 'I'm going to take you somewhere really fabulous,' he had said over the phone. 'After all, it's the second anniversary of the day we met. The fifteenth of August will always be special to me.'

'Oliver, you remembered! What a romantic you are!'

'You'll see just how romantic I am when I whisk you into the best restaurant in London. I had to fight to get a table there, so we mustn't be late. Look, I've got to go now, but I'll meet you at the City Bar at seven o'clock. OK?'

'That's fine. That'll give me just enough time to rush home, wash, change and do my hair.

'You promise you won't be late?'

'I promise.' Her heart had been full to bursting. I her wardrobe she had a knockout grey silk dress she had bought the previous week when it had called out to her from the shop window. Oliver had never seen it, but she'd bought it with him in mind and now he'd arranged this special evening.

She'd also bought him a wonderful anniversary present. A pair of expensive cufflinks, gold with a white enamelled design. She couldn't wait to see his face when he opened the box.

★　★　★

All day, she'd kept on top of her work and had warned her boss and her colleagues that she had to leave the office at five o'clock on the dot. That was early for her. She and Oliver had had words lately because she often didn't get away until at least seven o'clock and it was often even later, and he'd become sulky and accused her of placing more importance on her work than on their relationship.

Although neither of them had said it, this evening would be a sort of test of where her priorities lie. She knew she mustn't mess it up.

When five o'clock came, she'd cleared her desk and, after being on tenterhooks all afternoon in case something came up at the last minute, she'd flown out of the office as if she had wings on her feet.

Dashing into her smart, ultra-modern flat, she'd kicked off her shoes and thrown off her clothes, showered, washed and blow-dried her hair and had slipped into the gorgeous silk cocktail dress.

Then, just as she was standing in front of the mirror finishing off her make-up, her mobile phone had rung. She'd smiled and pressed the button, thinking it must be Oliver with some last minute surprise.

But the shutters came down on her smile as she recognised the voice on the other end of the line.

'Hi, Cassandra, it's Ted Ramos here.'

Ted Ramos was the president of her bank, her boss's boss, and the most important man in the company.

'Cassandra, I've got Felix Weisberger our US chairman here — we're having drinks before dinner — and a question has come up about your current project. I need you here right now, Cassandra.'

She'd looked at her watch. It was a quarter past six. 'But, I . . . I'm afraid I can't come, Mr Ramos. I've got a very important appointment.'

'*Now*, Cassandra.' His tone held an underlying threat. It was plain that, 'No,' simply wasn't an acceptable answer. But she could tell from his tone of voice that he was smiling as he spoke to her — smiling because Felix Weisberger was sitting opposite him and a forced bonhomie was essential during such negotiations.

'It won't take long,' he went on. 'I know you don't live far from the office. I've sent my driver round. He'll take you on to your appointment afterwards. I'll see you in ten minutes.' The line went dead.

She felt utterly powerless. In her world, being summoned by Ted Ramos was the ultimate accolade; it meant you were important, indispensable. Any other time, she would have been delighted.

But not that evening.

Her doorbell rang. She quickly scurried around grabbing her handbag, velvet jacket and the last bits of her make-up to finish off in the car. Maybe she could still be on time for Oliver. In the car, she tried to phone him but her call went through to his voicemail.

She checked the time again by her watch — the jewelled watch that Oliver had given her at their last anniversary meal, in Capri.

In no time at all, she was rushing into the lobby of her office building, feeling the tension grabbing at her throat as she jabbed the button on the lift to take her up to Ted Ramos's executive suite.

An excruciating half-hour followed. Outside, lights were coming on all over London as the night grew darker. She rapidly fired answers off to all the questions Ted Ramos and Felix Weisberger aimed at her, all the time watching the hands on the clock creep around to seven. It was like some form of torture. Finally, at five past seven, they let her go.

As she sped down the stairs, she felt her breathing becoming shallow.

Back in Ted Ramos's company car, she asked the driver to take her to the City Bar as quickly as possible and dropped her phone on the floor as her shaking fingers tried Oliver's number again. She was already late.

This time, thank heaven, he answered. But instead of his usual cheery, 'Hi!' Oliver's voice flatly asked, 'Where are you?'

'I'm so sorry! I'll be there in twenty minutes. I know I promised not to be late, but I really couldn't help it! Please, Oliver, have a drink or something. I'll explain everything when I get there.'

She was babbling, she knew it. Her hand clutched her throat as she listened to the awful, empty silence on the other end of the line.

Oliver had cut the connection.

It had taken Ted Ramos's driver half an hour in the heavy London traffic to reach the restaurant and, during every one of those thirty minutes, she could feel her anxiety mounting. She even thought of getting out and running to beat the traffic, but she knew that would just make things worse.

When she finally arrived at the City Bar, her heart was pounding, her legs felt weak and she'd had to rush into the loo to splash her cheeks and neck with water to calm herself, knowing that otherwise she would burst into tears and ruin the evening altogether.

The bar had been crowded with happy evening revellers. Smart-suited young businessmen, city girls, couples hand in hand, smiling, flirting, gazing lovingly into each other's eyes. And,

Oliver, sitting alone at a table, his face like thunder.

With her anniversary gift to him clutched in her hand, she'd walked over to the table and sat down.

★ ★ ★

Now, her mouth felt dry just thinking about that evening. She closed her eyes, not wanting to remember. Even more, she didn't want to recall the occasion of her second panic attack, which had happened almost eighteen months later and which had been far worse.

She'd thought that she'd put that scene behind her. She'd played it out so many times in her mind in the wee small hours of the morning that she thought she'd stopped thinking about it. But here it was again. The scene had shot unbidden and unwelcome into her mind.

And now she remembered vividly how she had stood, on her wedding day, her beautiful white satin dress cool against her ankles . . .

No! To allow herself to relive that day was madness.

She opened her eyes and shook her head.

When a soft, insistent nudge at her ankle forced her mind back to the present, she breathed a massive sigh of relief and picked up Smokey, cuddling his purring little body close to her.

The past was the past and the present was here in her own garden, in the sanctuary of Seaport which, thankfully, was a million miles away from the past. And from Oliver.

The present was where she wanted to be and the present was what needed her attention. She hadn't allowed herself to re-run those awful times with Oliver for ages. What on earth had prompted her to think of him now?

She frowned. *Adam Hawthorne*. He had been the catalyst which had allowed that Pandora's Box of memories to open.

She could have kicked herself. Yes, Adam was good-looking and about the same age at Oliver. Yes, she could be attracted to him. But he was trouble. In any case, even putting aside the issue of the TV series, if thinking of Adam made her think of Oliver, she was best scrubbing him right out of her thoughts. She had her home, her restaurant and now, her cat. That was everything she needed.

★   ★   ★

Then she remembered that she had invited, actually *invited* Adam to dinner at her restaurant that evening! Oh, well . . .

She was sitting deep in thought, toying with Smokey's ear when suddenly he started to scratch violently at it. When she looked closer, she saw that as well as several fresh little scratches, there were ugly scabs around his ears where he'd scratched before.

She jumped up, holding on to

Smokey and chastising herself for her self-pity. It was obvious the poor kitten had fleas or some other yucky and uncomfortable condition and something needed to be done about it.

Immediately, she sprang up from the step and headed back indoors to phone a vet, thankful for something useful to do that would get her out of this despondent mood. She would not let Adam Hawthorne and everything he represented grind her down.

★ ★ ★

She'd wondered if Smokey was a stray or whether he had an owner who simply didn't look after him. Now, seeing him scratch himself raw, she was determined to make him better and to give him the love he deserved. Just holding his purring, bony frame in her hands made *her* feel better.

As she didn't have a proper cat basket, she hunted out a shopping basket which had a cloth cover. He'd be fine in there for the few minutes it would take her to drive to Mr Swanson, the vet in the High Street. When she'd phoned, the veterinary nurse had said they were having a quiet afternoon and urged her to take the kitten straight round.

As she sat in the driver's seat listening to Smokey mewing beside her, she lifted the cover from the basket and stroked him to settle him down. The little creature needed her and she wasn't going to sit around moping.

As she negotiated Seaport's winding streets, she thought about the evening ahead. After the difficult confrontation they'd had that morning at the meeting, she would have phoned Adam to tell him not to come if she could have, but, of course, she didn't have his number.

Oh, well, she had plenty of other things to think about apart from him.

She had a business to run, a temporary waitress to find and a small cat to look after.

Adam Hawthorne could go and boil his head for all she cared.

Maybe he wouldn't even turn up tonight. But if he did, she'd certainly give him a piece of her mind.

A Lovely Evening

'You were right to bring him in to see us, Miss Waverley. He's a cute little thing isn't he?' Smokey stood on the vet's black-topped table, his tiny paws leaving moist impressions because he was sweating with fear. Cassandra stroked him to calm him down after the car journey which he obviously hadn't enjoyed.

'Do you think he's a stray?'

'Undoubtedly. No one has cared for this cat before you. See his fur? Long-haired cats need to be brushed every day to stop their fur balling. If these small lumps of matted fur were left unattended, they would gradually get worse and have to be shaved off. As it is, for a little 'un he's done a reasonable job of washing and caring for himself and if I just snip off these few lumps with some scissors, then there won't be too much damage done to his coat.'

In a couple of seconds the vet had snipped away the matted lumps.

'You'll need to buy a brush like this — we have some for sale outside in the waiting room — and use it every day. See, he really likes it. You'll have a friend for life there.'

'And what about his ears. Is it fleas?'

'Amazingly, he doesn't seem to have caught fleas yet. It's contact with cats or other animals which usually leads to fleas. Your little one here is obviously a loner, although he certainly seems to have taken to you.'

Smokey licked Cassandra's hand and stood up on his hind legs, lifting his head so she could brush the top of it.

The vet settled him down again and peered into his ears using a tube with a torch attached.

'His problem is ear mites. He could have caught them from his mother. They're quite common. But it's a good thing you brought him in so soon because, although not serious in themselves, the scratching can open the skin, leading to infection. I'll clean up his ears and prescribe some drops which you'll need to use for a month. We'll give him something to clear up any secondary infection and then he'll be as right as rain.'

'Thank you. He's a dear little thing isn't he?'

As the vet swabbed Smokey's ears he said, 'I can see he's already decided where he's going to make his home. Did you say you owned the Feng Shui restaurant down by the harbour?'

'That's right.' Cassandra picked up Smokey to comfort him after his ordeal and he nestled against her jumper.

'He's going to get well fed, then! He could do with a little fattening up. Just make sure you aren't tempted to feeding him too much or he'll become overweight. I often get obese cats in here who have to be put on strict diets. It's a shame, but you have to keep an eye on how much they eat, just the same as we have to keep an eye on ourselves.'

The vet rubbed his own slightly rotund tummy self-consciously.

'For now, though, I'll give him all the jabs he needs against things like cat flu and we'll give him a worming preparation. I'd advise you to keep him inside for a while until the vaccinations kick in.'

As Cassandra paid the bill, she browsed amongst the pet-related items for sale in the reception area and selected a carrying basket, a brush and comb and a tiny jewelled collar with a bell.

'There,' she said, looking at him all brushed and bejewelled as he peered out of his basket at the people walking up and down the High Street. 'From pauper to prince in one easy step. Let's drop in on Ellie so she can see how well you look.'

★ ★ ★

Ellie worked at the local estate agent's and waved to Cassandra as soon as she saw her walking through the door.

'So this is your little stray. He's a cutie.' Ellie and Theresa, who shared the desk next to her, crowded round to look at him and stroke him through the mesh.

'He looks thirsty,' said Theresa, making her way to the kitchen. 'I'll get him a saucer of milk.'

'Lucky the boss isn't in,' said Ellie as she opened the mesh door to the basket and Theresa placed the saucer inside. 'Fancy a cup of tea? We've just put the kettle on.'

As Cassandra gratefully drank her tea, Ellie looked at her with concern and said, 'You look worried. What's up?'

Cassandra's forehead wrinkled as she frowned. 'It's Megan, she's hurt her arm and will be off work for a while.'

'Oh, no, that's really bad news.'

'You can say that again. And to top it

all, I stupidly invited Adam Hawthorne to dinner at the restaurant tonight. I don't know what I was thinking of, but for a moment or two I felt pathetically grateful to him.'

Cassandra explained to the puzzled Theresa the problems she'd had with her car and how Adam had appeared to be a saviour but was in fact a wolf in sheep's clothing.

'It's bad enough that I invited him at all when I'd rather not see him again. But without Megan helping in the restaurant tonight, I'll have to do all the waiting myself. I won't even be able to sit and talk to him and the main reason for inviting him was that I'd hoped to get a chance to try to change his mind about using Seaport as a film location. Now, he'll assume I'm just being difficult and that I don't want to talk to him.

'But it's not just tonight's dinner that's a worry. I've got to get a temporary replacement quickly for Megan because I'll not cope for long single-handed.'

'I used to do a bit of waitressing,' Theresa said from behind her computer screen. 'Before I came to work here I was signed up to an agency. I wouldn't want to do it for more than a few nights because I already have to work weekends here, and a girl needs a bit of a social life! But, for a day or so I could help out. I'm free this week until Friday.'

Cassandra could have hugged her.

Then Ellie said, 'And as for tonight, since you've got the big bad wolf coming to dinner, I'd be very happy to come along and play chief waitress. In fact, I wouldn't miss it for the world!'

'Oh, would you?' Cassandra grasped her friend's hand and then went over and put her arm around Theresa. It felt as if the heavy cloud that had been hanging over her had suddenly cleared.

She walked out of the estate agent's with her chin held high and her grip tight and sure on Smokey's carrying basket. She marvelled at how, with the help of true friends, you can feel one minute as if disaster is about to strike, and the next as if all your problems are small ones.

★   ★   ★

On the way back to the car, since Smokey was sleeping peacefully, she popped into the pharmacy and picked up a new strawberry-pink nail varnish and matching lipstick. They also had a lovely black velvet bow on a clip which would look great keeping her hair in check. Finally, she splashed out on a bottle of expensive perfume.

Tonight, she wasn't going to be a waitress. Tonight, she was going to see what it was like being a guest in her own restaurant!

It was a long time since she'd been out to dinner with anyone. Should she wear the white dress with the pastel designs on it or the plum-coloured one with the autumn leaf motif? She'd covered her bed in half a dozen outfits. They seemed like old friends who she didn't see regularly enough.

Definitely the plum-coloured one, she finally decided, slipping it on and zipping it up.

She'd dried her newly-washed hair into waves, and put it into a ponytail, held back with the velvet hair clip.

After wearing her uniform of black trousers and white shirt every day, month after month, she felt wonderful to be dressed in *girly* clothes again.

She breathed in the perfume that she'd sprayed on her wrists. It was nice to be 'going out' again, and with a man. Even if 'going out' meant just going downstairs and even if the man was Adam Hawthorne.

'What do you think, Smokey?' she asked the kitten, doing a little twirl. 'Huh, you don't care what I look like, do you?'

She peered into the mirror at her reflection, at the glossy lips, and at eyes which looked wider with a stroking of dark eyeshadow. Suddenly she wondered why on earth it should matter to her what she looked like. After all, it was only Adam Hawthorne she was meeting and he was nothing more than a thorn in her side.

As she headed downstairs, she noticed that the light on her private phone was blinking, indicating a message on the answerphone.

Pressing the button, she listened, then felt herself stiffen as she heard the urgency in the young, female voice.

'Hi, Cass, it's me. How're you doing?' It was her younger sister, Sarah. There was a long pause. 'Um, look, sorry I haven't phoned in ages and ages. You'll be thinking I only phone when I'm in trouble. But this time things are really bad, Cass. I don't know what to do. I'm in such a state. Dave and I broke up. And . . . Well, something else awful happened, too. I don't know what to do. Well, I guess that's it, really. Sorry, but I really need to speak to you. Phone me. Please.'

The line clicked and went dead. Cassandra looked at the phone, then looked at her watch.

She needed to get downstairs to speak to Jorge about the last minute preparations for the menu tonight. Spending ages talking to Sarah — who was obviously in the throes of yet another of her crises — wasn't a good idea right now, but Sarah was her sister. And she sounded as if this time she really did have problems.

Cassandra had always had her doubts about Dave. He could be very unreliable and he and Sarah had been through a lot of rough patches before in their marriage. But then again, you could never see into other people's relationships; only the two people in them really knew the truth.

Cassandra picked up the phone and dialled. A wave of guilty relief washed over her as she heard Sarah's answerphone click in — 'Hi, this is Sarah. I'm not here but please leave a message.'

'It's Cassandra, Sarah. I got your message. Really sorry to hear about you and Dave. I'm in the restaurant until late tonight, but I'll phone you first thing tomorrow, I promise. Take care. Love you.' Cassandra put down the phone and rushed downstairs.

★ ★ ★

Waiting for Adam was purgatory. She couldn't settle to anything, especially as her mind now kept flitting to her sister, imagining all sorts of dramas.

When she'd gone downstairs, Ellie and Theresa were already there, looking smart and efficient. They'd spoken to Jorge and studied the menus and familiarised themselves with the cash register.

'Maybe I should take the night off more often,' said Cassandra as she sipped a glass of wine, smoothed her dress and peered out of the window.

'Well, we're enjoying ourselves, so you can have the night off as often as you want,' said Theresa.

Cassandra's eyes roamed around the restaurant.

'Those salt and pepper mills might need filling.'

'Done it,' answered Ellie.

'And I usually polish the glasses just to make sure they're sparkling.'

'Done that, too,' replied Theresa.

Ellie pushed Cassandra over to a small sofa by the bar and made her sit down on it. 'You need to take it easy and stop worrying about everything. Let me top up your glass, Madam, and for heaven's sake just relax.'

Cassandra took another sip of her chilled wine, just as Adam walked in through the door. She saw him before he saw her and she froze, her glass halfway to her lips.

Watching him as he stood in the doorway, tall and clean-shaven, his open-necked dazzling-white shirt — worn under a casually elegant black velvet jacket — revealing the top of a lightly tanned chest, Cassandra's stomach flipped as if she was going down in very fast lift.

In his hands, he held a bunch of white and yellow roses and freesias, tied

116

up with crinkly cellophane. The scent wafted over to her and she realised she'd been holding her breath. How long had she sat there like a statue, staring at him?

Then he was there in front of her. 'Hi!' He offered her his right hand to help her up from the sofa and held out the bunch of flowers to her as he said in a low, husky voice. 'A peace offering. You look stunning by the way.'

*　*　*

Stunned was exactly the way she felt.

She'd been so determined to do battle with him, to tear him off a strip for being the indirect cause of her humiliation at the public meeting. It was Adam's fault that Councillor Watson had attacked her. If it wasn't for his choice of Seaport as the location for the TV drama then she would never have had to stand up and say her piece in the first place. But here he was looking, quite frankly, more gorgeous than any man she had ever seen, and offering her flowers. He certainly knew how to take the wind out of a girl's sails.

Flowers! How long had it been since someone had bought her flowers?

For a couple of seconds, her legs wouldn't take instructions. Maybe it was the thought of holding his hand and yet there was nothing for it, it would be churlish not to accept the gentlemanly gesture. Out of the corner of her eye, she could see her two friends looking at her intently.

She put down her glass on the side table, reached out and allowed him to take her hand. As he touched her she felt herself blushing like a teenager. His hand was warm, slightly rough and immensely strong, and a tremor ran up her arm which seemed to electrify her legs into action. She got up and quickly took her hand away, accepting his bunch of flowers with the other.

'Thank you, they're lovely. I'll just put them in water.'

Ellie scooted over, took the bunch

from her and said quietly under her breath so that Adam couldn't hear, 'No, you won't,' and then a bit louder, 'I'll take those, Miss Waverley,' — *Miss Waverley? Since when had Ellie ever called Cassandra that?* — 'Please, take your seats.'

Cassandra felt herself being hustled over to the best table near the window and she sat down, feeling her hand still tingling from where Adam had held it.

He lowered himself into the seat opposite her, managing with difficulty to tuck his long legs under the tiny table for two. As he looked into her eyes, she wished that she'd had the tables made bigger — the closeness of the person sitting opposite had never been so apparent to her before. Or maybe it was just that being close to Adam Hawthorne was unlike being close to any other person.

'I hope you don't think the flowers are just to butter you up. I really did want to say sorry for what happened at the meeting.'

She'd wanted to rant and rave at him, yet now he was here, apologising, she found she couldn't do it.

'I did feel rather uncomfortable.'

'Of course you did,' Adam sympathised. 'Councillor Watson was way out of order, speaking to you the way he did. He more or less threatened you. I was really shocked by his attitude.'

'Then you don't know him very well.'

'You're absolutely right there. He did speak to me before the meeting and was as nice as can be. Now that I think about how mild mannered and matey he was, phrases like 'snake in the grass' come to mind.'

Cassandra couldn't help but smile at him. 'All I can say is, I'm glad you managed to work that out for yourself. Even though I know that phrase sums him up perfectly, if I'd told you that was my opinion of him, you might have thought I was simply protecting my own interests. Of course, I *am* doing that, too — I'm a businesswoman trying to survive in a competitive world. But he's an extremely slippery customer and I'm glad you saw that for yourself. One minute he can seem to be your friend and the next, if he doesn't like what you're doing, he's quite happy to stab you in the back. He has some powerful friends in this town. It's a small place, so he's a big cog in a small wheel, and he'll have made a note to get his own back because I've voiced an opinion that contradicts his own.'

'I hope he won't make life difficult for you.' Adam's dark eyes were heavy with concern.

'He might try. But I'm a big girl now. I can take care of myself.'

'Well, let's forget Councillor Watson. I've been looking forward to eating in your restaurant and taking some time out. Life's been a bit too busy lately. Can I order you a drink?'

'The house white's very good. I can recommend it. Last year I went on a buying trip to France and bought up most of the stock of a very small but top class vineyard.'

'Great!' Adam caught Ellie's attention and soon she brought over a perfectly chilled bottle. As they sipped the excellent wine, Adam listened intently as Cassandra talked him through the menu.

'The really special thing on tonight's menu is local oysters. I think they're the best in the world, but then I'm biased.'

'I'm happy to take your word for it. I certainly don't dine on oysters every night.'

They selected these as a starter, and a special beef dish with fresh green vegetables for their main course. As Adam started talking about some of the appalling places he'd been forced to eat when looking for location shoots, Cassandra found herself smiling more than she had done in a long while.

'You mean you saw a dead mouse in the corner of a restaurant?'

They had finished their oysters and the beef had arrived.

'That's right,' he said, 'its little toes were curled up. Then the waiter pretended he'd dropped a serviette on the ground and when he picked it up the mouse had mysteriously disappeared but the serviette looked as if it had doubled in size.'

Cassandra laughed and, as she watched his eyes crinkle into yet another smile, she realised she was actually enjoying the evening that she'd dreaded. She'd meant to try to dissuade him from his project but now she had to concede that what she'd needed this evening was to have some fun, not another confrontation. The thing that surprised her most was that it was Adam Hawthorne, of all people, who she was having fun with.

'That beef was terrific. Please pass my compliments to the chef,' said Adam. 'So,' he asked after they had placed their dessert orders, 'explain to me about Feng Shui. Isn't it all just some oriental mumbo-jumbo?'

'You could call it that but then you might just be accused of being horribly cynical and close-minded.'

'People have called me worse, I can assure you. But I will grant you that this place really does have a certain something about it. A really peaceful sort of ambience or atmosphere.'

As she looked around at her happy customers, chatting and enjoying the food, Cassandra said, 'I'm glad you think so. I've worked hard to make this a relaxing and enjoyable place to come to for a meal, but using the principles of Feng Shui to guide me made it easy, because that's what Feng Shui's about really, being in harmony with your surroundings. It's also about creating somewhere calm and productive, an oasis of peace away from the pressures of the outside world.'

'Your surroundings are obviously important to you.' It was the first time he had alluded to the fact that Cassandra's home and restaurant had become everything to her, and that he was possibly the one who might upset all that.

'They are the most important things

in my life at the moment. By trying to escape from my former lifestyle and from the city where everything had gone wrong for me, I've found a place which is really special, somewhere I can be happy.'

A long silence followed as if Adam was choosing his words very carefully. A sudden seriousness had descended on the evening.

'Can you really be that happy living alone? Did your plans never include someone else, someone special?'

She swallowed back a lump in her throat and her hand gripped the stem of her glass so tightly she felt it might crack. 'My plans might have included someone once but not any more. They say it is better to have loved and lost than never to have loved at all. They're wrong.'

The second the words were out of Cassandra's mouth, she wished she'd bitten them back. What was it about this man that made her drop her guard? He knew exactly how to reach her core, how to aim his questions like sharp-tipped arrows — once a policeman, always a policeman she reminded herself.

He looked pointedly towards her whitened knuckles and she self-consciously released her hold on the wine glass.

As Ellie hovered nearby, Cassandra said, 'Could I have coffee, please? Large, very strong and very black.'

'Cappuccino for me.' Adam steepled his fingers and leaned his chin on them, the picture of relaxation.

Cassandra braced herself for more questions.

'You were going to tell me all about Feng Shui.'

He was deliberately changing the subject.

★   ★   ★

Sipping the hot coffee, she felt it sharpening her up. 'Feng Shui is what gives this restaurant its atmosphere. If you can harness the earth's Chi or energy, whatever you like to call it, you can increase your success in all walks of life. Home, business, even *romance*.' She emphasised the last word deliberately. She wasn't going to have him thinking she was some bitter old maid who was afraid of the subject. True, romance was something she'd never contemplate again but that was none of his business.

'And *how* do you harness the earth's energy?'

'If you were really observant,' she batted back at him, 'you would see the signs all around you.'

'Enlighten me,' he challenged, spooning the froth off his cappuccino as if it was ice-cream, before sipping at his coffee.

Cassandra found his devastating looks distracting, but she knew her subject, she had studied it well.

★ ★ ★

Trying not to notice the way his hair flopped back on to his forehead as he

127

ran his fingers through it, she started talking, as if giving a lecture.

'Where a particular property is sited can affect the energy it attracts. The minute I saw this property I knew it had an excellent flow of energy around it. It faces south which is regarded as being the source of warmth and wealth. The trees behind the building and the hill going up to the town means that my little restaurant will receive support from these natural forces during troublesome times.'

Adam raised an eyebrow. 'Go on,' he said smoothly.

'The chair you're sitting in is a horseshoe shape, which wraps around you and is synonymous with the ideal living location. Being near the sea is also ideal — water gives great energy flow but you have to be careful with it. Clean, moving water is great, but stagnant and polluted water brings illness and bad luck.'

'And do you feel that my coming here has brought you bad luck?'

'That remains to be seen, doesn't it? I feel I've protected myself pretty well from ill luck. Those wind chimes hanging near the door are there to frighten away any unlucky Chi. And the mirror reflecting the cash register is designed to increase my business turnover. Even the fish tank over there is designed to attract wealth and prosperity. There are nine fish, eight are gold — the colour of money — while the ninth fish is black, absorbing any bad luck which might come to me.'

Adam looked over at the fish darting back and forth happily in their tank and said, 'Poor little thing. The black fish of the family.'

'I have a strong suspicion you're laughing at me.' Cassandra tilted her head. 'But you can't argue with the fact that the Chinese are fabulously success-ful in business. I first got interested in Feng Shui while I was on a banking trip to Singapore. I was booked into the Hyatt Hotel and on the way to dinner, our host told us how business at the hotel had been very poor until the positioning of the doors had been changed on the advice of a Feng Shui practitioner. Business improved and the hotel became one of the most successful in the area. You can't argue with results like that.'

'I'm not mocking you at all,' said Adam. 'We all try to bring magic into our lives in various ways. My wife was my bit of magic.'

'It's good that you can talk about her.'

'Oh, I like to talk about her. It's odd, but when you've lost a loved one, people think you can't talk about them. I had friends who would call around to check on me, make sure I was all right and try to look after me by bringing me around a meal or taking me out. But the one thing I was desperate to do was talk about my wife and yet they always steered clear of the subject. They thought talking about her would upset me. In fact it was *not* talking about her which upset me. And so did the way everyone seemed to be pretending she'd never existed.'

'It's difficult,' said Cassandra. 'But I guess people don't know what to say.'

'I can understand that they might find it awkward. But the best thing they could have done was to talk with me about the good times. And Jenny and I did have such good times.'

* * *

Seeing that he'd finished his coffee, Ellie, without being asked, came across and topped-up his cup.

'You haven't finished your dessert,' said Cassandra.

She realised with surprise that she didn't want him to go; didn't want the evening to end. Now that he had started talking about his wife, she wanted to learn more about his past. He had quizzed her, and now in her gentle way, she wanted to know more about him.

'Oh, don't worry, I have every

intention of finishing my dessert,' he said, taking a mouthful of summer pudding. 'Strangely enough this used to be one of Jenny's favourites. She grew loganberries and blackcurrants and raspberries in our garden and used them up by making lots of jam and summer pudding. The garden's gone to wrack and ruin now. I have a man who comes round to tidy it up when I'm away, but it's not the same. It needs someone to nurture and care for it rather than just keep it tidy.'

'What's your home like?'

'It's a nice, family-sized home in south London. Maybe I should have sold it, moved out, because there are too many memories there. But they're good memories. Why should I leave? It is a bit too big for one person, though. We'd always planned on a family, but it didn't happen. We thought there would be plenty of time for that.'

Cassandra's curiosity was burning inside her and she longed to ask what had happened. Had his wife succumbed to illness or an accident? She could hardly ask him straight out.

But although there was a sadness in his eyes, he seemed pleased to be talking about the past. He was a world away, his deep dark eyes that looked into the past were lit with golden flecks as he bathed in good memories.

Then, suddenly, Adam's gaze hardened. His eyes froze like a statue's. She noticed his hands which had been loosely holding his coffee cup were now balled into fists. 'We didn't have enough time together because I failed her. I failed to protect her.'

'What on earth do you mean?'

'I was a policeman,' he said through gritted teeth. 'An upholder of law and order. I was good at my job, one of the best of my rank, and I couldn't even protect the person who meant everything to me. I was guilty. Guilty of not saving her.'

'But what . . . ?' *Guilty?* That was a heavy word and a heavy burden to bear. Cassandra had so many questions bubbling up in her head. So many things she wanted to ask him, but there was so much pain etched into his brow which had furrowed with anger. Anger at himself.

Before she could ask the questions she wanted to ask — *What happened to Jenny? What did you do . . . or not do?* — Adam had got up from his chair and was taking out his wallet. It was clear he was putting a full stop to their evening.

'It's been a lovely evening, Cassandra, but I have to go now. I enjoyed it, really I did. Much more than I had imagined I would. I hope you did, too.'

'I did, Adam, very much. Please, you don't have to pay. This evening was on me, to say thank you for helping me out with the car. I won't hear of it.'

'And I won't hear of *not* paying. I've brought you a lot of trouble, I can see that. This place is lovely, you've made it fantastic, and it's your sanctuary. My coming here to Seaport has created only problems for you. The least I can do is pay my way.'

She opened her mouth to protest but could see that he wasn't about to give in. 'Well, thank you. You shouldn't have.'

'No hard feelings and all that?'

She got up, acutely aware of his hand on her back, steering her as they walked together to the entrance.

Outside, under the stars that glowed out of a dark sky, he stood facing her, so close that she could detect on the breeze the masculine scent of his lemon and sandalwood aftershave.

For a second they stood in silence; for a second she thought he might kiss her. And in a second the moment had come and gone, like the scent of the sea which wafted up the street on the night air.

'I'll no doubt see you around,' he said, backing away self-consciously. 'I've ordered a couple of books from your friend next door, Jasper Eames. I'll have to call by to pick them up at some point.'

'Pop in for a coffee, when you do,'

she called after him wistfully as he turned to walk away.

She watched as, broad shoulders hunched, fists buried in his pockets, he returned alone to his hotel, her heart aching to see his pain.

'Next time, coffee's on me!' she cried out. But her words had drifted away into an empty street.

Sarah's Tale Of Woe

It had taken hours for Cassandra to drop off to sleep. While she'd been taking off her make-up in front of the bedroom mirror, thoughts of Adam had crowded into her head.

Then she'd lain awake in her bed, curtains open, tossing and turning to the sound of distant waves and, staring towards the window had tracked the path of the moon across the sky, as snatches of their conversation played through her head again and again.

It was hardly surprising that, when morning came and she awoke to the sound of thumping on the door downstairs, she was startled into consciousness with a jump.

Pulling her dressing gown around her and stumbling down the stairs on jelly-like legs, she opened the front door thinking it must be an emergency.

'Sarah!' There stood her sister in faded jeans, a T-shirt bearing the logo of a recent pop festival, and a denim jacket. Wearing no make-up, with her short hair flat against her head and her eyes red from crying, Sarah looked a complete and utter state. She had a small suitcase at her side, and despair written all over her face.

'Oh, Cass.' She fell, sobbing, into her sister's arms. 'I didn't know what to do. I didn't have anywhere else to go. You've got to help me.'

In an instant, Cassandra was wide awake. 'Sarah, you look dreadful. How did you get here?'

'I hitched a lift. I've been travelling half the night. I had to sleep on a bench in a lay-by.'

'Hitched? Oh, you shouldn't. That's terribly dangerous. What if you'd come to some harm?'

Cassandra swept up her sister in her arms and guided her through to the kitchen, feeling the younger girl's shoulders shake with sobs.

'I don't care.' Sarah gulped and sniffed. 'The way I'm feeling, it wouldn't have mattered. Anyway, I was picked up by a very kind lorry driver with three teenage kids of his own. I was as safe as houses.'

Cassandra tore off a sheet of kitchen roll and gave it to Sarah who blew her nose loudly. 'I'll make coffee.'

* * *

Sarah leaned against the kitchen work-top, her tears gradually subsiding. 'Thanks for the coffee. Is there anything to eat? I'm starving.'

'Anything to eat?' said Cassandra, smiling for the first time. 'This is a restaurant, what do you think?'

Half an hour later, after eggs, bacon, tomatoes and toast, Sarah was sitting upstairs on Cassandra's sofa, feet curled under her, still looking drained but a little bit more like her usual self.

'It was just awful, Cass. I love Dave so much and yet we had this huge row.

He stormed out, didn't take his mobile phone and told me he wasn't coming back. Then the landlord came down and gave me notice to quit. I found out that although I've been giving him my half of it, Dave hasn't been paying the rent. Apparently he used the money to buy new gear for the band. I spent ages at work phoning his friends to find out if they'd seen him. I was distraught. I just want him back. I was desperate to speak to him. Then my boss called me in and tore me off a strip for using the office phone for personal calls.'

'Oh, Sarah, I hope you apologised.'

'I couldn't. I was too upset. And anyway, they've told me off before, given me what they call a verbal warning, then a written one because I've had to phone Dave before from work. The trouble is, he's gone off like this before.'

'Why?'

'I don't like the way he spends so much time with his friends. We've argued about it loads. We're married now, he should be spending more time with me. The thing is that when he goes to play gigs in pubs there are always loads of girls hanging around. Sometimes I wish he'd just get an ordinary job. Him being a musician and that, playing the guitar, girls just drop at his feet. You know how good-looking he is.'

Cassandra decided to say nothing. Apart from on his and Sarah's wedding day when for once he'd worn a suit, Cassandra had only ever seen Dave in ripped black jeans and a white T-shirt, looking as if he'd just got out of bed. She wondered how girls could even tell what he looked like, he had so much hair falling over his face.

But Sarah was right in that he seemed to be a bit of a girl-magnet, and Sarah had a fiercely jealous nature. As a child, and now as an adult, she'd strike up close relationships with people and expect them to be her friend exclusively, complaining if they wanted to go off and do their own thing, or spend time with anyone other than herself.

Cassandra bit her lip as she listened to her sister cataloguing the recent chaos that had engulfed her.

'The next thing I knew, my boss had sacked me. Told me I'd had plenty of warnings and that they couldn't run the business if staff were on the phone making personal calls all the time.

'Oh, Cass, I've lost Dave, my flat and my job all in one go. And after all that trouble last year with our Mum, I'm not sure if I can take it. What am I going to do for a living; where am I going to stay?' Sarah peered into her coffee mug hopelessly as if maybe she'd find the answers there.

All that trouble last year with our Mum, thought Cassandra. That had hit her hard, too, harder than she'd liked to admit at the time.

Even worse, after discovering the devastating truth about her own and Sarah's parentage, Cassandra had realised how much she wanted a family of her own.

It was painful thinking about it even

though she'd hoped she'd come to terms with it.

★ ★ ★

She felt herself go clammy at the thought of that period in her life and all that it had thrown at her. She'd hoped that Oliver would be the rock on which she'd build her future and that the two of them would not only have successful careers, but that they'd make a lovely home together and create their own strong family unit. She'd wanted two, maybe three children.

But first she'd found out about her mother, and then had come the awful split from Oliver.

At least she'd managed to pour her life and soul into the Feng Shui. At least she had the restaurant, but what did Sarah have? A dead end job in an office and now not even that.

Her sister sat on the settee biting her nails, looking desperate.

'Come on, love.' Cassandra put a

comforting hand on her arm. 'You can stay here for a while. I've done up the spare bedroom. I'd wanted to let it out to paying guests, because I need more income to be able to expand the Feng Shui. But you're welcome to stay for a week or two. In fact,' Cassandra began to brighten as she thought the problem through, 'I can even give you a job.'

'You! Give me a job?'

'Sure. You did a bit of waitressing work didn't you, in that pub where you met Dave?'

'Yeah, but that was a while ago and, anyway, I wasn't very good at it. I can't add up figures in my head and I used to get very flustered working out the cost of people's rounds.'

Cassandra remembered with a wince that Sarah hadn't lasted very long in the pub but immediately pushed the thought out of her mind. After all, she was desperate for help and Sarah was desperate for a job, so maybe it was the perfect solution.

Her younger sister's life was often

chaotic, but her heart was in the right place.

'Look, Sarah,' said Cassandra as she held her sister's hand which had finally stopped shaking. 'My waitress, Megan, has gone off sick with an injured arm. She's likely to be off for a week, maybe two. I can't promise you a job for any longer than that, but at least it might give you some time to get your head together, find a new flat and get yourself a new job. If you help me in the restaurant at lunch and dinner you can be contacting job and rental agencies in the mornings and after-noons. I can't help you with Dave, that's something the two of you have to work out between you, but I can help you with the practical things.'

'Oh, Cass, would you?' Sarah gripped her sister's hands as if she was hanging on for dear life. 'It would mean everything to me, everything.'

'That's what families are for, aren't they? Come on, let's get your bag into the spare bedroom and you can unpack and make yourself at home.'

'You're the best sister anyone ever had,' said Sarah, jumping off the sofa in her bare feet and running downstairs to fetch her things.

★　★　★

Later that morning, Cassandra called in at Ellie's estate agency, hoping her friend would be there. She was.

'Hi, how're you doing?' Ellie called brightly, looking smart in her business suit. 'I've got to take a load of mailshots down to the post office. I'm due my elevenses, so we could take in a coffee on the way.'

'That would be wonderful,' Cassandra agreed.

'You'll be OK here on your own, won't you, Theresa?'

'Fine, thanks. I need to do some shopping myself, so if you can cover for me later on, then I can cover for you now.'

Cassandra and Ellie delivered all the

letters to the post office, then settled down on one of the leather sofas at Cardini's coffee shop, comfortable in the steamy warmth, and ordered fresh coffee and croissants.

'So, how did your dinner with Mr Wonderful go last night? You two certainly seemed to have a lot to say to each other.'

'I guess we did and it wasn't at all like I thought it would be. It was weird, actually.'

'In what way?' Ellie crossed her legs and rested her arm along on the back of the sofa.

'Well, I was spoiling for a fight. I really wanted to tell off Adam Hawthorne for bringing me so much trouble and for potentially turning my life upside down. But I couldn't do it.'

'I'm not surprised.'

'You aren't?'

'No. I saw how you looked at him, Cassandra, and I don't blame you. He's gorgeous. And he couldn't take his eyes off you, either.'

'Rubbish.'

'It's not rubbish, it's true. Even though that restaurant was full last night, every time I looked over at the two of you it was almost as if there was no-one else there. You were so locked on to one another.'

Cassandra could feel a blush searing her cheeks. She hadn't realised that how she'd felt had looked so obvious. She shook her head to get the vision of Adam out of her mind.

'Anyway, I've got other things to think of now, just as potentially troublesome as Adam's film location agency.'

'Like what?' Ellie bit into her croissant, and brushed crumbs off her skirt.

'Sarah's turned up on my doorstep, looking for comfort and help.'

As they finished off their coffees and ordered top-ups, Cassandra related the events of the morning to her friend.

'Wow, that's rough on poor Sarah. I know she's not the most sensible person, and there's always something in her life going pear-shaped, but to have a triple whammy like that, losing your flat, your job and your husband all in one go — it must be a nightmare.'

'I know.' Cassandra gazed at the pictures of Victorian Seaport that hung on the coffee shop walls. 'I feel sorry for her, too, but I just don't know whether having her living with me is going to work out. Even if it's only temporary.'

'She should make a good waitress, she's bright and breezy and gets on with people.'

'Yes, she's all those things. But she's always been a bit flakey and forgetful. The trouble with Sarah is that her mind's always somewhere else. Usually on Dave.'

'Hmm. I know their relationship has always been a bit volatile, but that's just the way the two of them are. But why do you think things have turned so sour between them lately. Is it just normal newly-married settling-down stuff?'

'I wish it was just that, but I suspect it's something more.'

'Cassie, you know I'm always happy

to listen, and I don't want to pry, but there's something you're not telling me. I can see it in your eyes.'

'You're right. But it's a family thing. It's to do with our mother and it's put a strain on both of us over the past months — and on our relationships. It's really kind of you to be concerned, but it's something both Sarah and I have to come to terms with on our own.'

'No worries. Just remember, I'm here for you if you need to bend someone's ear. In the meantime, let's be positive about Sarah. She may be miserable for a while, but if what you've told me about Dave holds *true*, it won't be long before they're together again. It's always been a bit of an on-off relationship, hasn't it?'

'It has. I think the reason Sarah always goes to pieces when they have a tiff is that she knows Dave's the love of her life. And he feels the same way, too, I'm sure of that. In a way they're very lucky that they both need each other so much.'

'At the moment though, you and she need each other. Do you want either Theresa or myself at the Feng Shui tonight, or can you and Sarah manage between you?'

'If she's as good at learning the ropes as the two of you were, I'll be fine, thanks.'

★ ★ ★

The girls downed their coffees and went their separate ways. All day long at the Feng Shui, Cassandra wondered whether she might see Adam visiting the bookshop. But there was no sign of him.

Sarah did pleasingly well at lunch and dinner. They weren't swamped with customers and, apart from the odd moment when Cassandra caught her sister staring into space while diners were trying to catch her eye, she seemed to be trying very hard.

The only trouble was, Cassandra knew from past experience that Sarah always started off with good intentions which then had a nasty habit of going awry.

But the last thing she thought of as she made her way to bed that night was Adam. Where was he at that moment and what was he doing? Try as she might to forget about him, Cassandra had found herself looking up every time she heard someone come into the restaurant, wondering if it might be him and trying to fix a smile to her face when it wasn't. And every time the phone had rung, even though it gladdened her to take a fresh booking, she felt a dip of disappointment when it hadn't been his deep voice on the other end of the line.

★　★　★

Three days went by with neither sight nor sound of Adam. Cassandra hadn't told her sister about him but, after all, what was there to tell? He was just someone who had come into her life, disrupted it and was now sensibly keeping his distance.

Nevertheless, occasionally, when she was not in a reverie of her own, Sarah would ask, 'Is everything OK? You look so far away!'

Cassandra pretended that it was worry about the possible filming and the fall out from any publicity that was preoccupying her.

But it wasn't just because of Adam that she was on tenterhooks; she was becoming increasingly worried about the wisdom of ever employing Sarah in the restaurant.

As usual, her sister had started off full of enthusiasm but, the night before, as Cassandra had been pouring drinks for a party of six, she had heard the raised voice of a woman who was obviously not happy with the service.

'This is inedible!' The shrill voice had carried through the restaurant. 'I said I wanted my steak well-done and this is practically raw.'

Hastily passing round the tray of

drinks, Cassandra hurried across to smooth over the complaint.

'I ordered my steak well-done. This girl must have cotton wool in her ears.'

Sarah stood sullenly by, her lips pursed as if she was just about to say exactly what she thought of the overdressed woman with the fiercely red lipstick.

'I'm really sorry, madam. I'll get the chef to cook you a fresh steak immediately,' Cassandra said.

'Good. And mind you don't simply reheat the one I've sent back, I know that trick.'

'We wouldn't dream of it.'

Grasping Sarah's arm, Cassandra lead her firmly away.

* * *

In the kitchen, while Jorge quickly rubbed garlic, pepper and salt into a fresh steak and tossed it into a waiting pan, Sarah protested, 'She didn't make it clear she wanted it well-done. I was sure she said rare, but she was so busy chatting to her husband that I didn't want to interrupt and ask again. She sort of shooed me away as soon as I took the order. She obviously wanted me to go away as quickly as possible.'

'OK, but it's always as well to check rather than risk getting it wrong.'

Sarah stood rooted to the spot, her arms crossed and her mouth set in a stubborn line.

'Look,' urged Cassandra, holding a plate with salad out to Jorge ready for the new steak, 'I'll look after that table and you can look after my people. They've had so many cocktails, they hardly care what they're eating anyway. They'll cheer you up a bit! Please don't look so miserable!'

Sarah stomped off and there were no more incidents that evening but, after that day, Cassandra had the constant feeling that sooner or later there would be trouble with her sister.

★ ★ ★

One morning, Cassandra was helping Jorge make-up some desserts and hadn't seen Sarah since breakfast when she'd explained to her that, on days when they were going to be particularly busy, part of her wages were for helping out in the kitchen — and had said that there were gooseberry fools to be prepared that morning.

But now, as Cassandra sat topping and tailing gooseberries, with pints of cream around her waiting to be whipped, there was no sign of her sister.

Eventually, feeling anger building up inside her, Cassandra stomped upstairs to her flat to discover that Sarah was curled up on the sofa, phone glued to her ear, with Smokey on her lap, chattering away like it was a Sunday morning and there was no work on. Her short, spikey hair stood up unwashed and she hadn't even showered.

'Sarah,' Cassandra hissed. 'I've been waiting for you.'

'Got to go now,' Sarah said into the handset. 'Phone me later.'

'What do you mean, *phone me later?*' echoed Cassandra, hands on hips. 'If you really want a job here and if you want to go on staying here, then the only thing you'll be doing later is going downstairs and pulling your weight. Actually, sooner rather than later would be nice.'

Sarah hauled herself up sulkily, placing Smokey on the floor. He ran under a table and hid as the girls' voices got louder.

'You're so unfair, Cassandra. That was one of Dave's best friends, one of the guys who plays in the band. He knows were Dave is and he said he'd help to talk him round. I have to stay in touch. You don't know how difficult it is for me. All that stuff about Mum hit me hard. I need a family now. I need Dave and I to be together.'

'I do know how difficult it is.' Cassandra struggled to keep control. 'It's difficult for both of us. But I don't sit around moping. I've got a business to run and if you don't go downstairs and help out like you said you would, neither of us will have any wages coming in.'

'Oh, the business, the business. That's all you think about, you're obsessed with your work. You're turning into an old maid. No wonder Oliver left you. No wonder our mother didn't want us!'

The words rang in the still air like the sound of an anvil after it's been hit with a hammer. Cassandra turned her back on Sarah and bit her lip to keep from crying out. In an instant, Sarah had run over and folded her arms around her sister's bent shoulders. 'I'm so sorry! I didn't mean it. Please, Cassandra, forgive me.'

Cassandra took in deep breaths of air, counting; one, two, three. Her hands covered her face. Sarah had been right about her work. Was it happening again? Was she putting too much energy into her business at the expense of any possible relationship? Why on earth did she keep on doing that? Was that why

Adam hadn't been seen for days on end? Because she sent out vibes that work was her only passion? Or was it because the pain of being jilted had been too awful for her to risk it happening a second time?

'Cass, look at me please.' Sarah peeled Cassandra's hands away from her face and held them in her own small hands. 'I'm so sorry I said that; I couldn't be more sorry. Oliver was a fool, and our mother didn't want us because that's how she is, not because of anything we did. I've found it difficult to accept that and it's so much easier to blame anything or anybody other than admit our real Mum's not a nice person.'

'It's OK, Sarah,' said Cassandra. She looked at her sister, then smoothed back a lock of her hair. 'I've been on the guilt and blame trip myself a thousand times in relation to our mother. Let's not fight. Let's not take it out on each other. Life goes on and you have to make the best of it. Go and get yourself washed and dressed. There are about a thousand gooseberries waiting for us downstairs and they've all got to be magically turned into gooseberry fools by lunch time.'

'Of course.' Sarah managed a smile. 'I'll break the world record for showering and dressing. Promise.'

★　★　★

Sarah was as good as her word, and at lunch time she was efficiency personified. Once or twice, Cassandra spotted her out of the corner of her eye, taking her mobile phone out of her pocket and examining it for messages but, luckily, she stayed on the job until all the customers had gone.

'If it's all right with you, Cass, I'm going to sit down here, finish off the filter coffee and write Dave a letter. His friends knows where he's staying, but he's not answering any of my calls. He might at least get in touch with me if I write.'

160

'That's fine,' said Cassandra disappearing upstairs. 'I've got a few calls to make myself.'

When she got upstairs she immediately dialled Megan's number. 'Hi, Megan, how are you?' she asked, trying not to sound too hopeful.

'Bored out of my skull. I wish I was back with you. I miss being at work.'

'I miss you being here. It's been a bit of a nightmare. Ellie and Theresa, the other girl at the estate agent's, helped out the other day and they were great but they've both got other jobs. My sister, Sarah's, staying here at the moment and is giving me a hand.'

There was a pause. Although Megan had never met Sarah, she'd heard about her colourful, drama-filled life from Cassandra. 'How's that working out?'

'OK. For the time being.'

'You don't sound too sure.'

'All I'll say is that I'll feel much more secure when you're back here.'

'Thanks, Cassandra, that's really nice to know. It won't be long now. The doctor says another few days and then I can start using the arm. Daytime TV's driving me nuts; it's stewing my brain.'

Cassandra laughed and went back to her chores with a lighter step. But when she went downstairs to gather up the aprons and tea towels for washing, she noticed Sarah outside, pacing up and down the pavement, talking into her mobile, and her heart sank.

Adam Lends A Hand

At about five o'clock, Cassandra was checking through the fridge and writing up the specials of the day on the blackboard outside. They had some very fine fish in and were making an extra-special effort with that evening's dinner menu as the local sailing club had made a large booking. It was for a party of ten and they would be useful customers who — if their evening went well — could introduce a lot more of their friends to the restaurant.

Sarah was upstairs, but had promised to be down early to help.

As Cassandra wrote the last of the specials on the board — hazelnut roulade with fresh raspberries — she jumped as a deeply masculine voice behind her said, 'That sounds good!' And she turned to look up straight into Adam's eyes.

'Hi!' Suddenly aware of the fact that she'd been too busy to brush her hair since the frantic lunch time session, she put up a hand and self-consciously tucked a stray strand behind her ear.

With difficulty, she managed not to betray how pleased she was to see him.

In as matter-of-fact a tone as she could manage she said, 'I see you've been to Jasper's shop. Did you get the books that you wanted?' She indicated the carrier bag he was holding.

'Absolutely! Three histories of Seaport with great pictures. They're ideal for research. But I'm not just here to pick-up my books. I wanted to ask you about something important. Do you mind if we go inside?'

What could he possibly want from her? 'Coffee?' she offered.

'Thanks.'

They sat down by the window, gazing out at the sea in the distance.

'I have a very important group of visitors coming tomorrow. They're staying in Seaport for a while and I wondered if I could book a table for dinner tomorrow night? And also if you'd join us?'

'Me? Why?'

He focussed his gaze into the distance and then up at Cassandra.

'Yours is the best restaurant in town, far better than the hotel's and I want to make a good impression. Also, I need somewhere quiet and discreet where we can discuss the project in peace. These people are the decision makers from the TV company; the producer, the backer and one of the stars — Jemini Devane, I don't know if you've heard of her?'

'How could I not have? She was on practically every magazine cover last year when she starred in that award-winning play. I'd have to live on Mars not to know who she was.'

Cassandra could feel her heart sinking. Jemini Devane was young, gorgeous and successful. A small, waif-like creature with curves in all the right places, long dark wavy hair and full lips, she was the sort of fragile-looking, doe-eyed woman who men fell over themselves to protect.

Jemini would have turned heads whatever she'd decided to do, but being on TV, she was making quite a name for herself.

'I can understand why you want to eat here and I'm happy to take your booking. I need all the custom I can get. But why on earth would you want me to sit with you? I'll be needed to wait on the tables as usual.'

'Well, I thought you could provide them with some local knowledge. I know a fair bit about the area, but not everything. You might not have lived here for very long, but you're so enthusiastic about the place! If they have any questions, maybe you'd help me out?'

'But, Adam, you know my feelings about all this! I have huge doubts about how a major TV series might affect the way of life here! I really don't want them filming here. So I might muck it all up for you.'

'But I'm sure if you met these people they'd be able to persuade you they could film here without spoiling Seaport, even if the place does become much better known. After all, the Inspector Morse series didn't ruin Oxford.'

'Yes, but Oxford was already world famous before the cameras went there.'

She bit her lip. Although she didn't support his project, she wanted to be fair to him. Besides, it was true that if wealthy people from London started to think of Seaport as a good weekend destination it would do hers and the other small businesses here the world of good.

'OK, I'll do it,' she said reluctantly.

'I'm really grateful to you.' Adam looked more relaxed now, relieved in fact. 'And I'm sorry,' he continued, 'not to have been around for a while. I'm at a major turning point in this project. The next few days will be crucial. I've been busy writing up my report or I would have come around sooner to thank you again for such a wonderful meal the other night.'

★ ★ ★

Suddenly, as they were chatting, thunderous footsteps came clattering down the stairs. Sarah, her jacket half-on and half-off, clutching her handbag and mobile phone, almost ran into the tables at the bottom of the stairs.

'Cassandra, I've just had wonderful news. Oh, hello,' she said, realising she was interrupting, then went on, 'Cassandra, Dave returned my call. He said he's been thinking about me, he even said sorry at one point. He wants to get together and talk. Isn't that fantastic?'

'It is, Sarah, but I hope he doesn't mean right now. Not just before the dinner guests start arriving.'

She could feel her anxiety levels rising. Surely Sarah wouldn't do that to her? But then again, where Dave was concerned, Sarah was so madly in love.

'But, Cass, you have to understand! He's coming down here, all the way on the train. I can't ask him to wait till tomorrow, he was already on his way when I spoke to him.'

'Sarah, what am I going to do? The restaurant's going to be full tonight!'

'Can't you ring Ellie, or Theresa?'

'Ellie's taking her mother to a concert — they'll be arriving in London as we speak — and I don't have Theresa's home number. I've only ever contacted her through the estate agent's office and she'll have gone home already. Oh, how could you let me down like this?'

Sarah looked like a rabbit caught in headlights. Then Adam suddenly said, 'I'm sure I could help out.'

'You?' cried Cassandra. 'How?'

'Well, I'm wearing a white shirt and dark trousers. I reckon I'm dressed pretty much like a waiter. If it's just a question of being nice to people, delivering plates and taking money, then I'm your man.'

'I bet you've never waited on a table in your life.'

'You're right there, but I've eaten in restaurants often enough, and I've eaten at this one very recently. I know your menu. Hey, I'm a Libran! We take forever to choose what we want and, believe me, I studied that menu line for line when I ate here. So, how difficult could it be?'

'No, no way,' said Cassandra standing up and glaring at Sarah.

'Why not?' pleaded Sarah. 'I'm sure . . . ' She looked at Adam questioningly.

'Adam,' he supplied helpfully.

'Adam will be great.' Why not? Cassandra toyed with the question. Because I don't want to be beholden to Adam again? Because I'm frightened of being close to him for a whole evening in such a confined space?

Sarah's voice re-entered her consciousness. 'I was never any good at waitressing anyway. I really want to help you out, Cass, and I promise when I

170

come back I'll stay and be really, really good until Megan comes back. But just for tonight, I have to see Dave. It could be our last chance.'

Cassandra looked at her, at the hope and worry in her eyes and knew she'd have to say yes, and what's more that she'd have to let Sarah go with her blessing. Even if it did mean working in close proximity to Adam Hawthorne.

'Go on, then,' she conceded. 'Go and get him back. Have you enough money with you?'

'Yes.'

'And your mobile phone in case you need to ring me?'

'Yes.' Sarah's blue eyes danced with expectation and her feet wouldn't keep still, she was so eager to be out of the door.

'Off you go then, or you'll be late.'

Sarah hugged her tightly. 'You're the best sister, Cass.'

Then, with Sarah's spikey hair tickling her ear, Cassandra heard her younger sister say, 'With a sister like you to take care of me, who needs a mother, anyway?'

Cassandra turned away from Adam, quickly wiping her eyes and sniffing.

'Your sister's very sweet,' he said gently.

But she pretended she hadn't heard him. 'Right, Adam, if you're really going to work for me tonight, you'll have to be on the ball.'

'Yes, ma'am.' He stood to attention and she couldn't help thinking how devastating he looked when he smiled.

'I'll show you how the till works and where the wines are kept. Oh, and introduce you to the most important person in the place — Jorge, my chef, of course.'

★   ★   ★

Cassandra was getting the first customers settled in when she heard a strange noise coming from the kitchen. It was a sort of barking, hollering noise which, when she went through the door, she discovered was Jorge doubled up with laughter.

'Sorry ma'am,' Adam winked at her. 'Your chef and I seem to have the same sense of humour.'

Eyes wide in amazement, as soon as she'd delivered the order to Jorge, Cassandra pulled Adam aside and said, 'How did you do that?'

'Make Jorge laugh, you mean?'

'Absolutely. He's the most inscrutable person I've ever met. I've barely ever been able to get him to raise a smile. He's great, and a wonderful chef but how on earth you made him laugh, I don't know.'

'Easy,' answered Adam with a twinkle in his eye. 'Jorge has hidden talents. Did you know he was a tango champion back in Buenos Aires? We talked about boys' stuff. You wouldn't understand.'

★ ★ ★

The rest of the evening went like magic. With amazing self-confidence, Adam wowed the group from the yacht club, flirting just enough with the women to make them feel flattered, and joking with the men.

He remembered every order, topped up glasses with such aplomb that they seemed to serve twice as much wine that evening and, with the customers who made it clear they wanted to chat, Adam was knowledgeable on every subject under the sun.

He was also discretion itself, so that when a young woman who was clearly nervous and on a first date dropped her bread roll on the floor, he slid along next to the table as if nothing had happened and whisked it away, delivering another one with all the skill of a magician.

As Cassandra closed the door behind the last customer and put up the *CLOSED* sign, she looked at the empty wine bottles and debris left by the satisfied diners and said, 'You don't want a permanent job as a waiter, do you?'

Adam sat down at one of the chairs, stretched his long legs out in front of him and grinned. 'I don't know about that, but I think this bottle of house red needs to be finished.'

'Mmm. Just one glass would be great to round off the evening.'

'The yacht club said your restaurant is just the right size for their committee's Christmas do. The chairman wants you to send him the Christmas menu — although he said they'd have to book the whole restaurant for the evening.'

'That's wonderful. A Christmas booking this early in the year! I don't know how to thank you.'

'You could come for a walk with me on the beach. It's such a beautiful night and, after being inside all evening, it would be wonderful to get some fresh sea air.'

★ ★ ★

The evening was so still that they walked straight out in their shirt

175

sleeves, down to the deserted sands. It was a perfect night. The moon, huge and round and the colour of clotted cream, was reflected in the water which lapped up against the smooth sand. It was so quiet that Cassandra felt they were the only two people awake in the world. She caught her breath at that tiny sensation.

'What do you say to a paddle?'

'At this time of night?' Cassandra laughed.

'Why not? Don't your feet ache?'

'Like crazy.'

'Let's do it then.'

★ ★ ★

Rolling up their trouser legs, they took off their shoes and left them on the sand and, laughing at what might happen if they forgot where they'd left them, they picked their way over scattered mussel shells down to the water's edge.

It felt so right to Cassandra to be

with Adam. They say the best things in life are free, and this feeling of togetherness was priceless.

They wandered for five minutes in silence, listening only to the water splashing around their feet, until they came upon a log that had been washed up at the water's edge.

'Let's sit,' said Adam and they perched on the sea-worn wood, their faces bathed in moonlight.

He kicked his feet, splashing in the water. 'I haven't felt as good as this since before Jenny died.'

'Your wife.'

'Yes. I hardly ever have the chance to say her name these days. It feels strange to say it now, it feels almost as if she was from a different world altogether. They say the past is another country don't they?'

'Is it too painful to talk about what happened to her?' Cassandra suddenly had a burning need to know all about it. He'd talked about how guilty he felt, and yet she couldn't possibly see how a man who appeared so caring could be guilty of anything.

'It would be painful if I was talking to the wrong person. But with you, here, right now . . . ' he said, taking a deep breath. 'Jenny and I had been married a few years. We were planning a family. We had our whole lives ahead of us.'

He stared out into the distance at the miles of calm black sea.

'I was doing well in my police career and we had a lovely home. Then I began working on a project to break up a family gang of ruthless criminals. These guys would have sold their grandmothers for a few quid. They were into every scam going that could make money from good, honest people. The gang consisted of a father and four sons and they were responsible for many of the thefts in the area, handling stolen goods and running a protection racket by scaring local businesses into parting with cash in return for keeping them 'safe'.

'We observed them for ages, keeping

the whole operation secret. But they weren't just downright evil, they were clever. So clever that their accomplices were always the ones who were caught. Never the big boys. Never the father or the sons!'

Adam paused, briefly, possibly thinking how far away all that evil was from this tranquil moment in time.

Cassandra had the feeling that any malice he might have once felt had been dealt with. He had somehow plumbed the depths of his being to get to a place where he didn't have to feel hatred. Hatred can crush the spirit and Adam definitely wasn't a man who was crushed.

'We caught them in the end. At least, we caught the father who was the ringleader, and the eldest sons. They were jailed but there was nothing that would stick to the youngest son, Darren. We knew he was involved but we couldn't get the evidence to prove it.'

'You don't have to go on.'

'No, I want to tell you.'

On impulse, Cassandra put a hand softly on his arm, feeling his strong muscles through his crisp white shirt. 'Go on.'

Adam looked back out to sea.

'After the trial had come to an end and the publicity had died down, we went out one night, Jenny and I, with one of my colleagues, Steve, who'd also worked on the case, and Steve's wife.

'We'd all been to the theatre, then out for a meal. It was late. Steve was driving us all home and we were travelling along a dual carriageway when he suddenly yelled at me to look in the rear view mirror. We were being followed. Closely. Dangerously closely. Steve put his foot down.

'I told him not to go too fast, but he panicked. I hadn't realised how wound up he'd been by the trial. I should have seen the signs. He was my best friend. He was on the edge and I hadn't spotted it.

'I told him to calm down, but he

yelled back at me that he thought it was Darren driving the car that seemed to be chasing us. Then the car gained on us again, and we could see for certain in the mirror that it was Darren. Steve stamped his foot on the accelerator and lost control.'

There was silence, apart from the whisper of the sea stroking the sand.

'Jenny was next to me. She was killed instantly, the doctors said. She felt no pain. She looked as if she was sleeping. It was a freak accident. Apart from Jenny, we all walked out with just cuts and bruises. But it should have been me. She was innocent, she had nothing to do with any of it and I failed to protect her.'

'You're wrong.' Cassandra's voice rang out into the deserted night. 'There was nothing you could have done. It was like you said, just a freak accident. There are accidents that just happen; nobody can foresee them and we have to accept them.'

He turned to look at her. 'You're

sweet, Cassandra, and good. I saw you with Sarah; you wanted to make things better for her, and I appreciate you trying to make things better for me but I'll always know that I failed my wife; failed the family we would have had together. I'll always feel guilty about that.'

She had never before seen the sort of hopelessness she glimpsed in his eyes. She stroked his arm gently.

He turned back to look at her, and she dropped her arm saying, 'I wish I could help in some way.'

'You are helping.'

'How?'

'I need to focus on my work, on projects that take me away from the past. I need to be busy. You've certainly kept me busy tonight. Come on, let's walk for a while, down to the end of the bay.'

An Unexpected Kiss

They stood up and started walking again, their feet sinking into the damp sand. After a while, Cassandra broke the silence. 'The new TV series and a night helping me out might keep you busy, but you can't keep running for ever, Adam. You're still young. A family of your own should still be part of your plan. Home should be the place you go to relax and be you.'

'No. I'll never settle down with another woman, not while I have all this guilt within me. But what about you, Cassandra? Shouldn't settling down be on your agenda, too? I don't see any lucky guy waiting in the wings. Isn't there anybody?'

'Me and families don't seem to mix.'

'You seem to be doing a pretty good job with your sister.'

'That's because we have to keep

together. We don't really have anyone else but each other.'

'What about your parents?'

'Oh, yes, we've got parents.' She laughed hollowly. 'Too many, actually. But when it comes to parents, quality is what you want, not quantity.'

'You've lost me.' Adam had stopped walking and was looking deep into her eyes, one eyebrow raised questioningly. He was standing so close, she could feel his breath on her forehead. He put his finger under her chin and made her look up at him.

'What do you mean, Cassandra?'

She paused for a second, wondering if he was going to kiss her. But Adam hesitated, sensitive, waiting. When Cassandra resumed walking, he walked alongside her.

'When I was about ten years old, and Sarah almost nine, we were playing in the house one day. Our mother was in the garden and our father was at work. For some rebellious reason, we decided to sneak into the study where we were never allowed to be on our own. It was our mother's special place and it was always kept immaculately tidy. But not only had we been foolish and naughty enough to go in there, we'd taken our beakers of orange juice with us and left them standing on the bureau.'

Adam and Cassandra had reached the end of the beach by now, and turned around to head back.

'We'd been in there for quite a while, taking turns to sit at Mum's bureau and play teachers, when Sarah accidentally knocked over her beaker of juice, which dribbled down into the drawer where my mother kept her documents.

'I was terrified. She was a strict disciplinarian and I was desperate to hide the fact we'd breached her rules. I took the papers out of the drawer and wiped them desperately with a cloth. I couldn't help but notice the writing on some of them as I tried to dry them. But then I came across some old documents that mesmerised me and that I read again and again, although I couldn't quite take in what they meant.

'In these documents, Sarah and I were mentioned but we were given a different surname. The word 'adoption' was also mentioned several times. I was so absorbed, I didn't see the woman we'd always thought of as our mother coming into the room.

'She was absolutely livid. Because she was such a cold, strict woman, we'd always been a bit scared of her, but this was terrifying. She shouted at how ungrateful we were and how by snooping you were always bound to find out things you were better off not knowing. I guess I'd always felt that she was a bit more distant than our friends' mothers were towards them, a bit more brittle. She wasn't cruel or harsh or anything but she wasn't as soft and gentle as them. Now that I had learned she wasn't our birth mother, her attitude towards us seemed to make sense.'

★ ★ ★

As they walked back down the beach, Cassandra had the feeling that Adam wanted to put his arm around her. But he held back and just kept walking very close, his head down listening, as they slowly approached the path they had taken on to the beach.

'In my childish mind I began to fantasise about what our real mother was like. I envisaged her as sweet and cuddly and warm. All the things our poor adopted mother wasn't. What I later realised was that, just as she didn't measure up to our idea of the perfect mum, so had *we* failed *her*. She had wanted picturebook perfect children and neither I, with my gawky bookishness, nor Sarah, with her naughty and scatterbrained nature, fitted the bill. She did her best by us but there had always been this unresolved tension, because she'd tried to change us into the children she thought we ought to be.

'Anyway, as we grew older, I became desperate to meet my birth mother. I idealised this person I'd never met who I was sure had only given us up because of tragic circumstances. I convinced myself that she had bitterly regretted parting with us and had been searching desperately for us ever since.

'Our adopted mum was very understanding. She could have been bitter about my quest, but she gave me all the details I needed to seek out my birth mother.'

Adam and Cassandra had reached the spot where steps climbed up from the beach and on to the harbour wall. Wearily, she went up a few steps and then sat down. Adam stood before her, his eyes on a level with hers, waiting for her to go on, looking at her face, bathed in moonlight.

'Sarah and I were both in our early twenties when we finally tracked down our birth mother. We both sat hunched over the phone in the flat we were sharing as I dialled her number. When it rang, this confident voice answered. Her voice conjured up visions of tea parties on English lawns, pony clubs and judging at gymkhanas. As I falteringly explained who I was, there was a long silence. I had expected exclamations, tears of happiness, raw emotional joy. I was so young and so naïve. Instead, our mother lowered her voice — it sounded muffled as if she had put her hand over the phone. I couldn't understand why she suggested we meet in a park. Why hadn't she suggested her home or at least a café or a restaurant?

'But when we did meet, I understood why, and every expectation I'd had was shattered. Like a big beautiful bubble my hopes popped and disappeared. Our birth mother was embarrassed by us. She had a new family, a husband who was a lawyer and a son who she was desperate should never find out about us. Ever since she'd given us up, she'd been dreading us contacting her. She was frightened we would upset the peacefully floating cruise her life had become.

'I'd always imagined that she'd been

poor and struggling when she'd given us up for adoption but she hadn't been. She'd lived in a grand house with a well-to-do family but her father — our grandfather — didn't want us around. We were the product of a brief teenage marriage of which he'd never approved. Our father had been her family's gardener — what a cliché! I've no idea where he is now and, to be honest, I've decided it's probably best not to try to find out! Anyway, our mother ran away, married against her family's wishes and ended up living in a flat in a poor area. Of course, it didn't take her long to decide that wasn't what she wanted. When her father offered to take her back, giving us up was the price.'

'How are things with your adopted mother now?'

'They could be worse. I try to make it up to her.' Cassandra raised her face to him and tried to smile.

Adam brought up his hand, placed it under her chin and turned her face towards him.

'Poor Cassandra,' he said. 'Poor, brave Cassandra. You're so strong and I'll bet you don't even know it.'

Before she understood what was happening, he had placed his lips on hers, warm, firm and caressing. His hand slid protectively around her waist and she found herself falling, melting into his kiss, holding his firmly muscled shoulders as her head tilted back. It was as if he wanted to make everything better, to heal all the hurt she had carried with her.

Her stomach flipped over and her heart beat so hard she thought it would shatter. As she reached up to touch the soft curls at the nape of his neck, she felt his lips press harder and more insistently against hers, then he pulled sharply away.

In a moment he had released her, as if he had suddenly come to his senses.

Seeing her dismay, Adam reached out and took her hand, helping her up from the step. But then, as soon as she was standing, he pulled away.

His kiss had been so sudden, she had been taken by surprise. Her head was in a whirl and she doubted her legs would carry her. In silence, they wandered back to the Feng Shui.

But he didn't hold her hand as she thought he might. As they walked, she glanced at him only to see a worried frown on his face. Was he regretting kissing her? Had he acted in the heat of the moment and was he now wishing he could turn back the clock?

As they stood outside the door to the restaurant, she couldn't bear the silence.

'Adam, I . . . '

'Please, Cassandra. I shouldn't have done what I did there. I wasn't thinking.'

He grasped her shoulders and held her at arm's length, fixing her with an intent gaze.

'I'm not right for you. Please forgive me.'

'But — '

'Let's not spoil the friendship that we have. I shouldn't have been so foolish, I was an idiot. I can still come here for dinner tomorrow night with the TV people, can't I?'

'Why, of course! You're always welcome. But — '

'Then I'll see you tomorrow.'

In a moment he was gone, leaving her standing alone. And totally confused.

★ ★ ★

The next day, when Cassandra told Ellie and Megan that the film people would be dining at the Feng Shui that evening, she suddenly had no shortage of helpers clamouring to be waitresses.

Sarah had called to let her know that she and Dave had stayed overnight with the friends who'd been putting him up since he'd stormed out.

'I'm so sorry I can't be there, Cass, it sounds really exciting. All Dave's friends think Jemini Devane's a babe. I'd love to see her in the flesh. But it's great to hear that Ellie can stand in, and that Megan is well enough to come

193

back and take the orders, even if she's not ready to carry heavy plates. I'm sure you'll all cope. And things are really cool here.'

'It's good to hear that.' Cassandra was lying on her bed with Smokey snuggled up against her chest, nuzzling her neck. As she toyed with the kitten's ears, she wondered if she and Sarah would ever have more than a tiny grey cat to look after between them. A stable home and children seemed a world away although, hopefully, it was a little closer now for Sarah.

'So you and Dave have managed to patch up your differences?'

'I hope so,' Sarah chirped. 'We've done more talking this last twenty-four hours than we have in months. It's really cool. It's almost like it was when we first started going out. We got some pretty heavy stuff aired. He can't stand my being so jealous and reckons I need something other than him to focus on. So, I'm thinking of taking a teaching qualification. I've never done anything with my degree in English and he reckons I'd be good at teaching. If I got into that, then we could settle anywhere in the country; maybe find our own place somewhere property prices aren't so high. What do you think?'

'I think that sounds wonderful. Will you be coming back here to stay again?'

'If things go well, then I'm afraid I'll just be back to collect my stuff. I'm sorry, Cass, you've been so great, but if I sign up for my teaching qualification now, then could start next term. All this upset has been good in a way. It's made us think about planning the future.'

'Don't worry about things here. They're sorting themselves out.'

But were they? Adam's kiss had completely blown Cassandra away. It had been so unexpected and yet, she realised, she'd been waiting and hoping for something like that all evening. How many hours in the day did she spend thinking about Adam? Most of them, she realised. He filled her thoughts for almost all her waking day.

But nothing would ever come of it. He had told her as much, and she knew her heart was locked after Oliver's betrayal. And yet . . .

Her little flat above the restaurant seemed so deserted on mornings like this. She thought of Sarah, so full of hope and plans for the future, and Cassandra could see herself in several years' time, still here, still waking up in this same bed, on her own.

She heard the doorbell ringing. It would be Jorge, come to get things ready in the kitchen as usual. With heavy steps, she hauled herself out of bed realising that she had never, never been this late before.

★　★　★

Seeing Adam again when he arrived that evening was torture. He looked every inch the arty professional and was devastatingly handsome in smart jeans and a grey cashmere sweater.

'There she is,' breathed Ellie. 'There's

Jemini Devane. Oh, my goodness, she's gorgeous isn't she?'

She was. Every head in the restaurant turned and there was a sudden hum of excitement.

Cassandra wished she could have hidden behind her waitress uniform but, today, she was playing at being a guest again, and her summery green dress with tiny pink flowers which had seemed so appropriate when she'd put it on, now felt saggy and dowdy.

Jemini stood out like a bright butterfly, in a tailored, peach shift dress which finished well above her knees to display her perfectly shaped legs. Petite, but with an impressive amount of cleavage on show above the low V-neckline of her dress, and a pair of expensive dark glasses, she looked every inch the young starlet.

'You must sit next to me,' she purred, fluttering long curled lashes at Adam. 'I'm dying to hear about this new series.'

The rest of the lunch party — a

middle-aged man with a deep tan who was apparently the backer providing much of the finance for the series, a younger man and a bespectacled woman — all sat down as Ellie took their drinks orders.

Adam started the discussion by telling them all how he'd come across Seaport and why it was so ideal for the project. He took the earliest opportunity to introduce Cassandra.

'Cassandra Waverley owns the Feng Shui. It's the best restaurant around. But she's a woman of many talents. She used to be a structurer in a bank.'

'I've no idea what that is.' Jemini was looking at Cassandra down her pretty nose. 'Banking bores me terribly.'

Cassandra's words died on her lips and, although she caught an encouraging smile from Adam, she fixed her concentration on unfolding her napkin, aware of how dowdy she must look against the bright butterfly sitting opposite.

'My brother is a structurer,' the

female producer whose name was Ann Somer cut in, and she gave Cassandra a broad smile. And with a sideways glance at Jemini, she asked, 'From what he tells me, it's fascinating work. Why did you give it up?'

Cassandra and Ann chatted while Jemini ignored them, monopolising Adam and the financier, Jed Michaels. Cassandra caught snatches of the actress's tinkling laugh as she said, 'I'm off to do a series in Italy in the autumn. They're going to put me up in a flat in Rome all on my own. If any of you wants to visit, I'd be happy to let you have the spare room.' This was said with her chin resting on her hand, her wide eyes gazing at Adam.

More than ever, Cassandra wished she'd been able to fill her usual role of waitress that evening. That way she'd have been able to eavesdrop and then fade into the background. Sitting here was purgatory, trying to hold her own with these people who were on first name terms with actresses and writers and all sorts of other celebrities.

She sat on the edge of her seat. There wasn't a relaxed bone in her body. How could Adam have put her through this ordeal? It was plain that Jemini Devane had set her sights on him and from the way he was smiling and making conversation, they'd obviously known each other for some time.

For goodness' sake! Now Jemini had her hand resting on Adam's as she laughed at one of his jokes. Cassandra looked away. How could he have kissed her only the day before in a way that took her breath away and then today, subjected her to this? By the time dessert came, she couldn't wait to escape.

At long last, after coffee, they all started to get up and gather together their things.

They were the last guests in the restaurant.

'It was a wonderful meal, Cassandra.' Ann Somer shook her hand. 'And this town is a real find, so tucked away.

Thank you for giving me a little bit of the history of Seaport. The harbour is wonderfully atmospheric; how clever of you to have chosen somewhere with such enormous potential as the location for your restaurant.'

Meanwhile, Jemini gave her a cursory, 'Thanks,' and linked her arm through Adam's, urging him towards the door. 'These heels are so high, I need a little support from a strong man,' she giggled, tugging him away and he barely had time to say goodnight to Cassandra.

★ ★ ★

'Phew, thank heavens that's over.' Cassandra slumped into her chair and Ellie came rushing over to sit beside her. Megan, after helping as much as possible had gone home early, tired out by her first night back at work.

'How did it go? I only caught bits of the conversation here and there. I didn't like to eavesdrop too obviously.

I so envied you — imagine! Sitting around and chatting with TV people.'

'It was awful, absolutely awful.'

'No! How could it have been?'

'That's because you're naturally bubbly and sweet and they would have loved you.'

'But I'm sure they loved you, too.'

'They thought I was dull and boring. I could see it in their eyes and in the way they'd ask me a question, just to be polite, and then their attention would wander as I was answering. They were no more interested in a dull, unglamorous lump like me than they would have been interested in a sack of potatoes.'

'That's rubbish, Cassandra! You're a successful restaurant owner and you were a hot-shot banker, once. You're really interesting and you don't need to be glamorous in a false way, because you're a natural beauty.

'You're far prettier than Jemini Devane will ever be. She wears so much make-up she's almost wearing a mask, and her hair looks as if it's been tortured into shape. And what's more,' Ellie leaned forward to whisper as if they might have been overheard, even though Jorge was the only one left to hear them, 'I'm not even sure if that famous bosom of hers is real or it's sort of, you know . . .'

'What?'

'Manufactured. All the magazines say she's had plastic surgery. That sort of thing's just bizarre, and so narcissistic.'

Cassandra's eyes widened. 'Heavens, if I'd known, I'd have sneaked a better look. But I was too busy feeling nervous and out of place. I just wanted to crawl away under my stone and get back into the kitchen, where I'm safe.'

'You're safe here. You've made this place lovely and welcoming. I love it here; it's calming, it's peaceful, and it's the most wonderful place to relax. You're a hundred times better than Jemini Devane any day.'

'Well, she may have thousands of fans, but at least I've got one.'

'And a very loyal one at that.' Ellie

hugged Cassandra, immediately making her feel better.

Cassandra wished she could have told her friend about Adam's kiss. Yesterday it had seemed terribly exciting and important, and she'd intended to tell Ellie all about it. But after seeing him with Jemini Devane tonight, she felt utterly confused and not a little hurt and foolish.

Ellie left shortly afterwards and, exhausted, Cassandra showed Jorge out and went up to bed.

As she went to close the curtains in her little bedroom, she heard a familiar tinkling laugh and looked out of the window. There, walking down the street in the moonlight was Adam, with Jemini Devane hanging on to his arm. The others had obviously gone on ahead and left the two of them to walk the circuit of the harbour alone together, before they also headed off to their hotel.

Feeling a lump welling-up in her throat, Cassandra swiftly closed the curtains, wanting to shut out what she'd seen. In fact, at that moment, she felt as if she never, ever wanted to see Adam Hawthorne again.

★ ★ ★

Cassandra had just folded thirty napkins into the shape of water lilies, and had carved thirty carrots into the shape of fans. Her usual record for this was an hour and a half but, today, she had completed the whole lot in under an hour. Amazing what you could achieve when you were angry.

Last night she'd gone to bed thinking how duplicitous Adam was and, this morning, the first thing that shot into her head was a picture of him and Jemini laughing together as they walked arm in arm down the street.

She wondered whether Jemini might even have been laughing at her. She certainly seemed the sort of girl who'd make a point of laughing at any other female who didn't plaster on make-up, use gallons of hair products and wear her skirts short.

Hrrmph. Cassandra would wash the floor next. She'd probably break her record for doing that, too, she was so wound up.

She filled a bucket with steaming soapy water and flung open the door, because already the day was becoming hot.

When the phone rang, she was brandishing a mop which had been wiping the tiles so fast that, if it hadn't been wet, would have burst into flames.

'Feng Shui Restaurant?'

'Is that you, Cassandra?'

It was Adam.

'Yes, it's me.' She leaned on the mop, hand on hip.

'Oh, good. I remember you telling me a while ago that you had a room to let? Well, I'd like to rent it.'

An Unexpected House Guest

The colour shot into Cassandra's face like red wine spilt on a white napkin.

'You?'

'Yes, me. Why not?'

Because . . . because of lots of things. Because I don't want you around. Because you're trouble and I wish you'd never come into my life. Because just the sound of your voice makes me blush like a teenager and that's not good.

'Well, I don't know. It's . . . '

'It's vacant, isn't it?'

'Well, yes.'

'Great! I'll bring my stuff around later this morning. The trouble is, Jemini travels with such a vast entourage, and she's got her stylist and a photographer coming down today. When she saw the beach and the old Victorian lighthouses, she thought it would be the ideal spot to do some publicity shots. I thought there'd be enough room in the hotel for everyone, but a lot of the rooms are pre-booked because the Harbourne Music Festival's starting today. So, there's no room at the inn for poor old me.'

Cassandra racked her brain for a reason to say no. But there simply wasn't one. Sarah had made it plain she wasn't coming back to stay; the extra money would be useful and besides, Adam had helped *her* out on more than one occasion.

'OK,' she said weakly. 'See you later.'

Suddenly, the wind had been knocked completely out of her sails.

A while later, when Jorge wandered through, he gave her a strange look. He'd found her sitting there, door opened, floor half-mopped, wearing old jeans and out of shape T-shirt, her hair wilder than it had ever been, staring into space.

She finished off the restaurant floor,

then went upstairs to air the guestroom and change the sheets; moving Sarah's bag into her own room until her sister came back to collect it. As she did so, the phone rang again.

'Sarah, hi, how are you?'

'I'm fine,' said her sister sounding more relaxed than she had done in a while. 'Are *you* OK? You sound kind of stressed.'

'I am. Adam Hawthorne's asked if he can rent the spare room.'

Cassandra took a moment to collapse on the bed, it would do her good to talk to Sarah about this.

'Adam? He's that great-looking guy who helped out the night I left, isn't he? He seemed very respectable, Cassie. What could be so bad about him staying?'

★ ★ ★

Cassandra explained about everything that had happened between herself and Adam, and in particular about the night on the beach.

'The thing I don't understand, Sarah, is why on earth he would want to come and stay here, away from all the action. Jemini made such a play for him last night and, I have to admit it, she is beautiful. So why would he be the one to offer to give up his comfortable hotel room to be out on a limb here?'

'Cass, you know, sometimes, for an intelligent woman you can be very dim.'

'Thanks. Any more compliments you want to shower on me?'

'It's true. Has it never occurred to you that he actually likes you better than some overdressed, over made-up, full-of-herself bimbo? She might be glamorous but you shouldn't underestimate yourself. You're bright and feisty and really pretty in a way that doesn't need tarting up.'

Cassandra peered at herself in the mirror.

No, sadly, Sarah was wrong. The reality was that Cassandra could never match up to Jemini. All she could see staring back at her was a woman who looked as rumpled and crumpled as her sister's unmade bed.

She was also aware that her skin was a little too rosy from the day she'd spent in the sun at the boot fair, whereas Jemini's complexion appeared flawless — albeit with the help of some expensive foundation.

'It's kind of you to say — ' began Cassandra but Sarah stopped her in her tracks.

'It's not kind, it's true. He kissed you because he really wanted to and he'll want to again. Your trouble is, that you're so eaten up inside by what Oliver did that you can't believe anyone could like you for yourself. Maybe it's time you forgot that particular experience and started trusting people again.'

'I don't know what you mean. I don't have a problem with trusting people.'

'Don't you? You trusted our Mum then you found out she'd been keeping the adoption from us. You trusted our birth mother to want us back then you found she didn't. But just because people let us down doesn't mean we can't find anyone to trust, or that they won't make us happy.'

'Thanks for the amateur psychology.' Cassandra was aware that her voice was bitter, but this was her younger sister for heaven's sake, and look what a mess *she* was always making of things.

'I know what I'm talking about,' Sarah said earnestly. 'Believe me, I've been there myself with Dave. I've had my doubts but I was wrong. We're working it out and it feels so good to have someone to rely on.'

Cassandra felt as if she were being twisted inside. She'd come here to build her sanctuary, to get away from tough times. The Feng Shui had been the perfect distraction and now it had been invaded by Sarah, by Adam, by Jemini Devane, by people who'd turned all her carefully constructed peace and tranquillity into a whirlpool that she was stuck in the middle of, going round and round.

'Look, Sarah, I have to get the room

ready. Thanks for phoning. Was there something you wanted?'

'Only to say I'm coming back some time to pick up my stuff. As I don't know exactly what our plans are at the moment, is it OK if I just pop around when Dave and I get the time to come to Seaport?'

'That's fine.'

'See you soon then.'

* * *

When Adam arrived, he had one small suitcase and a laptop.

'You'll find the room's really basic.' Cassandra had had a chance to shower quickly and put her hair up. Her black shirt, simple linen skirt and silver flip flops were plain, but there was no point trying to compete with Jemini, so why bother?

But he was delighted with the room. 'It may be basic, but it's wonderful. You're very clever at putting things together. The blues you've used in here are so restful and the little desk in the corner is ideal for getting the last part of my report done. I think Jemini did me a favour! This is a much better atmosphere to work in than a busy hotel.'

He turned around and Cassandra realised she was standing too close to him for comfort. She moved back a step, needing to keep her distance.

It wasn't going to be easy having Adam living under her roof.

'I'm glad you like it. I have to prepare for the lunch customers now. I'm sorry I can't hang around.'

She was aware of the troubled look on his face but she couldn't help being abrupt. It was agony being near him when she knew his heart so definitely lay elsewhere. For a few minutes, she stood in her own bedroom to recover her composure before going downstairs and, as she looked around, she decided that now would be a good time to start decorating in there. It would keep her busy, and she could still be in the same house as Adam, but keep her distance without seeming rude.

She'd go to the hardware store and get a roller and brushes that very afternoon. She'd paint the room entirely white, including the old floorboards, and would make curtains and a duvet cover out of some pretty material that she'd been hanging on to. The fabric had a pattern of yellow primroses all over it, and would bring a feeling of sunshine into the room.

* * *

That afternoon, after covering the bed and the few bits of furniture with dustsheets, she started painting. Smokey ran around underneath the dustsheets, but she didn't have the heart to shut him out as he was having such fun.

Finally, he settled down in the doorway and just watched her.

First she painted the walls, which took all afternoon, then, desperate to finish before customers started arriving for the evening meal, she put the roller on a long pole and attacked the ceiling with gusto. It was much more difficult doing the ceiling than the walls, and she found she really had to push upwards hard to cover the slightly uneven surface. In particular, she had to pushed the paint really hard into the hairline crack that she was so fed up with looking at when she was lying awake, trying to asleep.

She finished just in time to roll up the dustsheets and clean her brushes before she was due downstairs, but the room looked clean and bright and she felt a hundred times better.

Once she'd changed and had gone down to the restaurant to join Megan, Cassandra mused to herself that, thankfully, she hadn't seen Adam all afternoon. He'd muttered something about taking Jemini to look at some possible scene locations. For a moment, she visualised the two of them in Adam's car, sitting side by side, and a wave of discomfort passed over her. Then again, she reminded herself, she'd given Adam the cold shoulder that afternoon, so she'd no right to feel jealous.

★　★　★

The next morning, she was up early as usual and was standing in the kitchen of her flat in her blue silk kimono, cutting bread for her toast. She looked up to see Adam coming through the door in his jeans and a baggy T-shirt.

Immediately, she wrapped her kimono more closely about herself and did up the belt in the tightest knot possible. Why hadn't it occurred to her that, of course, he would assume that the room was on a bed and breakfast basis like the hotel?

But she couldn't expect him to go out to find something to eat at this time of the morning. There was nowhere open this early in Seaport.

As he stood opposite her in the kitchen, she asked, 'Tea or coffee?'

Her mouth felt very dry for some

reason. Perhaps it was the sight of him looking tousled and sleepy and extra gorgeous.

'Always tea for me in the morning.' He smiled a devastating smile.

She concentrated hard on the tea cups, fumbling, finding it difficult to place them in the saucers.

'Toast, cereal? I can do you a full cooked if you want.'

'Whatever you're having.' He looked at the bread. 'Actually, toast would be great. I don't want to put you to too much trouble.'

She sawed away at the loaf while he leaned up against the door watching her. She wished he wouldn't.

'Cassandra?'

'Mmm?'

'Have I upset you in some way?'

'Of course not. I'm a bit busy at the moment that's all.'

He looked doubtful and not a little thoughtful and then moved to stand beside her. She felt his warm hands through the blue silk as he gripped the top of her arms and turned her to face him.

She could feel her cheeks blazing.

'Is it because of that kiss the other night?'

'Of course not.' Her answer came out in a flat voice because she didn't want to betray the emotion swirling beneath her words. She couldn't look at him though.

What if she looked at him and he saw the truth in her eyes? The longing for him to kiss her again. What if he saw that and still pushed her away from him? It would be too much to bear. There was no way she could give even a tiny part of her heart to a man and then find it discarded because he really wanted someone beautiful and successful like Jemini.

Cassandra had convinced herself that Adam's kiss had been intended to comfort her, because he felt sorry for her. It had meant nothing more than that.

When he released her she felt relief

and extreme sadness all in one go.

He sat down at her kitchen table and she went back despondently to taking slices of bread from the toaster, buttering them and placing pots of jam on a tray. This really wasn't going to work for very long. Just being in such close proximity to this man, in such a domestic situation, was almost too much to bear.

* * *

Maybe it wasn't just Jemini's beauty and success that attracted Adam. Maybe it was because she wouldn't make demands on him, wouldn't look for commitment. Jemini was not a settling down kind of girl.

And from what Adam had told Cassandra about himself, he would never settle down again either. If he wanted a simple no strings attached liaison, Jemini was the ideal woman. They were made for each other.

Cassandra watched Adam stretch,

looking wonderfully like a big cat, a panther or a tiger after a long sleep.

'What are your plans for today?' She did her best to make her voice light.

'I've got to organise a boat to take us all out for a tour around the harbour. While they're here, the production people want to suss out some of the shots they might be taking from the sea. Do you know of anyone who owns a suitable boat?' Adam crunched into a slice of toast liberally spread with marmalade.

'Jasper Eames does, next door. He doesn't go out in it much now, he's too busy in the shop, but he keeps it shipshape if that's not too much of a pun. His brother, Sam, often takes people out in it. He generally does trips from the harbour down the coast to Fretwell. It's pretty there. In fact, you could just as easily use Fretwell as your setting. There's a much smaller population there; less people to object to your plans.'

As soon as she'd said it, she wished she hadn't. Although she was still opposed to the filming, it seemed churlish to harp on about it while Adam was her paying guest and he was so near to clinching this deal which obviously meant so much to him.

His face was suddenly serious. 'You still don't want this TV series to go ahead, do you?'

'What do you want me to say? Meeting your production people for dinner convinced me even more that it's a bad idea. People like that, people like . . . well, just people who are interested in promoting themselves and their interests won't think twice about the wellbeing of the local community.'

'Actually, you may well be wrong there. I was talking to Jed Michaels, our financier, about your concerns. He may be a ruthless money man but he likes Seaport and he liked your restaurant. He said the crew could fill up your restaurant every day, breakfast, lunch and dinner. He'd also like to do a lot of filming in quaint shops like

Jasper Eames's. They'd have to clear out all his stock of course — it would be ideal for the shots which take place in the local chandler's store, but he'd pay handsomely for all the disruption. He is keen to put something back, you see. Maybe that'll change your view of things.'

'It would be lovely to see the restaurant full every day, and I'm sure Jasper would like to see his takings go up, but — '

'But,' Adam smiled, 'you still think it would turn Seaport upside down, eh?' He got up to take his dishes over to the dishwasher. Then he headed out of the kitchen to make his way back upstairs. 'I can't make it a perfect deal for you, Cassandra, but I can try to make it better than you thought. I'm doing my best to please everyone.'

She leaned forward and said, 'I know you are, Adam. I know.'

★ ★ ★

Adam said he'd be in his room most of the morning because he needed to work on his report.

Cassandra quickly tidied the small kitchen and went to get dressed ready to face the day.

She was just about to head downstairs to the restaurant when she heard a loud knock on the door. She was mystified as to who could be calling so early.

Running downstairs, she opened the door to find Councillor Watson, ruddy-faced, standing on the step.

'May I come in?' he said in a way which was more a command than a question. In fact, she couldn't stop him as he'd already crossed the threshold and had pushed passed her, to stand in the middle of the restaurant with his arms folded. His eyes seemed to be everywhere. She'd never liked him. He reminded her of a fat rodent, sniffing around in everyone else's business.

'What can I do for you?' She didn't offer him a seat or a coffee. There was no air of conciliation about him after their public argument at the meeting the other day.

'I understand you've got in pretty thick with the film people.'

'I don't know what you mean by pretty thick, but they have eaten a meal here, if that's what you're referring to.'

'And you've been seen around quite a lot with that location bloke.'

'Yes, I do know him.' What Councillor Watson obviously didn't know was that Adam was staying upstairs in her spare room. 'What's it to you? Or are you vetting everyone's friends now?'

Strutting through the restaurant as if he owned it, Councillor Watson made his way towards the back door and looked out at her garden area. 'Nice little place to expand into, this, isn't it? I see you've already made a start on the garden. I guess your next move will be to look for planning permission to extend your premises.'

Cassandra started to get annoyed and a little frightened by his probing questions. What was all this about?

'I'm sorry, I wish you'd get to the point. What do you want here? Is this an official visit of some sort?'

He laughed, an unpleasant, guttural sound which came from somewhere in his over-large belly. 'No, Miss Waverley. It is not official. But I do mean business. I'll get to the point. I hear you're getting pretty friendly with those TV people. You know I'm in favour of their drama series being filmed here and, quite frankly, I'll move heaven and earth to make sure that's what happens. You seem to have some influence with them so I'm asking you to make them welcome.'

'And if I don't?'

'It might matter a lot to you and your little business. Let me tell you something and let me tell you straight.' His face was round and red and ugly. 'If you don't change your tune, you might very soon find that things get difficult for you around here. If you want to expand you'll need planning permission and I happen to have a lot of influence on the planning committee. What's more, I've looked into your little business and I find your liquor licence is coming up for renewal. You may well find, young lady, that if you don't change your tune, your renewal request is unsuccessful.'

'On what grounds? There's never any trouble around here from my customers. You know that.'

'Do I now? I think I could find half a dozen people who would swear the opposite.'

'You wouldn't.'

'Just try me.'

'Try you at what Councillor Watson?' The voice which had interrupted them, strong and direct, was Adam's.

Neither of them had heard him quietly make his way down the stairs.

'Mr Hawthorne!' Councillor Watson's eyes were wide with something which Cassandra strongly suspected was fear. Adam looked and sounded every inch the ex-policeman.

Watson backed away towards the door. 'I didn't know you were here.'

'Obviously not,' Adam stated. 'Actually I happen to be staying here, in Miss Waverley's extremely nice guestroom. It's part of her growing business. A business which I am sure will continue to thrive and prosper and which you, I am sure, wouldn't want to jeopardise in any way.'

Councillor Watson looked for all the world like a fox that was facing the farmer's gun after being caught raiding a chicken shed.

'I'd better be going.'

He scuttled to the door.

Then, just as he was about to turn tail and run, Adam stood in his path, blocking his escape and locking him in a steely gaze.

'And please bear in mind that I heard every word of your conversation with Miss Waverley. I doubt very much whether your fellow council members would support your bullying tactics. You wouldn't want to be responsible for giving the council a bad name, would you now?'

With that, he stepped aside, politely ushered Councillor Watson into the street and shut the door.

'Are you OK?' Adam came over and stood close to Cassandra.

'Yes, but that was not funny.'

'I really have caused you nothing but problems, haven't I?'

She smiled weakly. 'Nothing I can't deal with. Besides, there's a sort of ying and yang effect.'

'Sorry?' Adam looked mystified.

'It's an oriental theory about the universe and there being an opposite to everything. Dark and light, day and night. What I mean is, that although your coming here may have presented problems, you've always done your utmost to put them right. Like the time you stepped in to do your best-waiter-in-Seaport act and like just now. You defended me Adam, and you protected me.'

'I guess I did. Surprising really,' he said in a self-deprecating way, 'given my terrible track record for protecting women.'

Cassandra knew that memories of his past were still haunting him.

'You're wrong, Adam. You're too hard on yourself.'

His brow furrowed. With a thoughtful look, he made his way back upstairs, leaving her hoping that maybe she was getting through to him.

Cassandra Does Some D.I.Y.

Their paths crossed very little during the course of the rest of that day, which was fine so far as Cassandra was concerned. As it was, she found herself going about her work like an automaton for, try as she might, she could not get thoughts of Adam out of her mind.

But, not only did he keep himself to himself during the day, there was no sign of him during the evening, either, and she realised with a lump in her throat that, of course, he would probably be dining with the production people — and Jemini — at their hotel.

She'd given him a key and told him he must come and go as he wished but she found she could not sleep until, late that night, she heard his key being turned very gently in the lock, followed by the sound of his footfall on the stairs as he came up to bed.

After that, she found she could snuggle up with Smokey and fall into a heavy sleep.

* * *

At breakfast the next morning, Adam looking more relaxed than of late, and sat hugging a mug of coffee. Cassandra cooked bacon, eggs and toast and realised how much she enjoyed having him around. Normally, this time of the day felt a bit empty to her. The rest of the time, the Feng Shui was so lively and bustling.

'Penny for them?' she asked Adam as she passed him his breakfast.

As usual he tucked into his food with gusto. 'I was just thinking that, since I've nearly finished my report, it'll only be a few days until I find out the production company's verdict. If they give Seaport the go-ahead, then I'll probably be staying around for the filming.'

'Oh.' Cassandra managed to keep her voice light. 'Right.' It sounded as if she didn't care and yet she found she cared so much she couldn't speak.

'If they turn me down, at least you'll be left in peace.'

She concentrated on her plate, as if it needed very careful consideration. Then, suddenly, into the silence came a shuddering bang from above them which sounded as if the roof had caved in.

* * *

Cassandra jumped out of her skin. 'Heavens, what was that?'

Adam sprang up from his seat and sprinted upstairs two at a time.

She leapt up after him and gasped in horror as she saw him open the door to her bedroom, letting out a huge cloud of dust that engulfed him.

'You've just decorated this room, haven't you?' he said once he'd stopped coughing.

'Yes.'

In front of her was a scene of devastation. A great slab of plaster the size of a door had fallen from the ceiling and now lay half on the floor and half across her bed. The amount of dust and debris was indescribable.

Cassandra's first concern was for Smokey. She looked around from left to right and started to call his name frantically. She could feel tears welling up in her eyes — she couldn't bear it if he'd been hurt — he was so tiny and so vulnerable.

'Is this who you're looking for?'

Adam had had the presence of mind to look in the lounge and there, lying contentedly on the sofa, eyes as wide as saucers, was one small and completely untroubled kitten. Cassandra wrapped him in her arms and went back to survey the scene of destruction in her bedroom.

'Looks like this was an accident waiting to happen. These old lathe and plaster ceilings are extremely heavy and they weren't built to withstand the sort of vibration we get now from the traffic that passes by. I'm afraid your bit of innocent painting must have pressed on the ceiling and dislodged it.'

Cassandra didn't know what to say. Everything in the room looked as if it was covered in the fallout from a volcano. What with everything else lately, it felt as if her sanctuary was literally falling about her ears.

A voice penetrated her thoughts. 'I said, do you have any black bags?'

'Sorry, sorry. Yes, I do, in the cupboard in the passageway where I keep the vacuum cleaner.'

'Good, we're going to need that, too.'

'You don't need to help me with this, Adam. It's my problem.'

'I want to help you,' he said. 'Come on, it looks worse than it is. If we both work on it, and if our little friend here stays out of the way — ' He picked up Smokey and popped him back inside the lounge, carefully shutting the door, ' — we'll have it sorted in no time.'

Adam was so methodical and so thorough. With the two of them working together as a team, what could have been a disaster was turned into a mere inconvenience.

'I really do appreciate your help,' said Cassandra as she bundled up the duvet cover and bedding to take downstairs to wash. 'I think I'd have gone to pieces if you hadn't been here.'

'Well I was. Thank goodness.'

'At least once I've changed the sheets I'll still have a bed tonight.'

'You can't sleep in here,' said Adam.

'I can't?'

'No way. What if the rest of it comes down? You were lucky it didn't happen at night. No, I insist you move into the spare bedroom with me. This is your home, you can't be left in danger. Do you have a camp bed?'

'Why, yes, but I can't move in with you.'

'Why not?' A smile crept across his features.

'Because, well, because.'

'There's nothing else for it. You have to be on site to look after the restaurant, I can't get another room in town until the music festival is finished. You can have the big bed and I'll have the camp bed. We'll be fine.' He raised an enigmatic eyebrow but she was sure she could see amusement twinkling in his eyes. 'I promise you I don't snore.'

★ ★ ★

The whole time they were setting up the camp bed, Cassandra was trying to think of a sensible reason to object to his plan. She could never say what she really felt. *You're too good-looking, and I can't bear the thought of you being in Jemini's arms one minute and trying to kiss me the next. What's more, you'll never be mine. Even although you flirt with me all the time.*

The last thought caused her cheeks to redden so much that she felt they might sizzle. She knew his flirting didn't mean anything, and she wanted him to stop it. There was only one thing for it. She must tell him about what had happened with Oliver. She must explain how much it meant to her not to get too close to another man. If he knew how high the stakes were for her he would back off completely.

It wasn't his fault that he didn't know the devastating effect he had on her. As it was she was sure he had no idea how far she was falling for him. Circumstances were pushing them together but she needed to do something to push them apart.

'You're looking very hot, Cassandra. Here, let me finish that off. There, it's all ready for tonight.'

'Adam, I want to say something to you.'

'Do you? I need to be getting off soon. I'm meeting Jed and Jemini for lunch.' He looked at his watch.

This just didn't seem the right time and place to tell him about Oliver. She needed to talk to him somewhere quiet, where they wouldn't be distracted.

'Did you say that tomorrow you'd be going out in a boat along the coast, past Fretwell?

'That was the place you mentioned as a possible alternative to Seaport, wasn't it? Well, I must admit that if there's any possibility the backers might reject Seaport then I want to have sussed out Fretwell so that I have an alternative up my sleeve. But I have a sneaky feeling that this is a grand plan you're working on to get me to change the location.'

'Maybe. It's just that I wondered whether you'd like to drive over there this afternoon, after lunch, to see it before you take the others? There's a really wonderful picnic area by the sea. We could take a light dessert with us — some strawberries.'

'OK.' He looked at her doubtfully, as if not quite sure what she was up to. 'I've got to hand it to you for persistence! You really don't want the film to be made in Seaport, do you?'

She couldn't possibly say that what was on her mind right now had far more to do with him than with the filming. That she was scared of falling for him and that she had to stop it happening.

'Um, let's just say I think you ought to see Fretwell.'

'OK. I could be back here in time to set off at around two o'clock?'

'That sounds fine.'

*   *   *

The weather was gorgeous on the short drive to Fretwell, with the sky a clear blue, and only a hint of sea breeze. It was an even quieter place than Seaport and they managed to get a parking space near the beach. Walking up from the tiny marina, there was a narrow path which led to a stretch of grass overlooking the sea.

Cassandra spread out the rug she'd brought while Adam surveyed the view.

'What do you think of the place?' she asked.

She opened a punnet of strawberries which they ate with tiny sweet powdery meringues that had been left over from the lunch menu that day.

After she'd eaten her share of dessert, she stretched out on the grass and lay back, looking up at the sky.

Adam had been sitting up but suddenly flung himself down beside her. On the small car rug, he felt dangerously close.

'Fretwell's very pretty, and bits of it might do for the TV series. But it doesn't have half the sense of history about it that Seaport does. I'm surprised you think it might be an alternative.'

'It was just a long shot.' She could feel the warmth of the sun, and the warmth of Adam's shoulder next to hers. As she closed her eyes, she suddenly felt his hand close over hers. For a few blissful seconds, she savoured the feel of the sun on her skin, the warm breeze on her face, and Adam's hand holding hers. Then, like a bad dream it all changed as she wondered whether he had held Jemini's hand in the same way.

'Adam.' She sat up, pulling her hand quickly away. 'You've been so good to me, helping with various things. Despite us being at odds in one way, you've helped me in so many others.'

He lay on his side on the ground, his head resting on his hand, looking at her earnestly.

'But, you remember when you told me about your wife, and that you feel so guilty about her death that you don't see how you can ever form another meaningful relationship? Well, I can't ever go down that route again, either, but for different reasons.'

'Cassandra you're vivacious and you've got so much to offer. You don't know how much you've helped me to see that maybe I'm looking at things in a way that is too black and white, too yin and yang to use your phrase. I'm beginning to think that a relationship is something I might be able to — '

She stopped him instantly. 'I have to tell you something, Adam.'

She didn't want to hear that he'd fallen for Jemini. Yes, he'd kissed Cassandra and held her hand, but she knew that was just because he felt sorry for her. She knew he wanted her as a friend but surely not as anything else. She knew she wasn't a patch on Jemini who had literally turned men's heads that night in the restaurant. Also, Jemini was so much more emotionally available. She'd flirted outrageously with Adam, she wasn't frightened of a relationship.

'I have to tell you what happened between Oliver and I.'

'What did happen?' He sat up and was so close, she could smell the aftershave he always wore.

'Oliver was the love of my life. I'd never before met anyone I felt so in tune with. We were so much on the same wavelength, I'd even find that I often knew what he was going to say before he actually said it. He worked in the same field as me, in banking. And yet there were things he didn't understand about me.'

'In what way?'

'What he didn't seem to understand was that I wanted to do well in my career for the two of us, so that we could have all the material things we wanted. I was incredibly ambitious and whenever he thought I was putting work in front of his needs, he got jealous. For a while, he just used to get grumpy and not tell me what was wrong. I think he felt embarrassed to admit he was jealous of my success.

'Anyway, we had a terrible argument one night when I was late for an important anniversary meal. That taught me a lesson and I was careful not to make the same mistake again.

'I thought we'd patched things up because a short time later, he asked me to marry him. He wanted a big wedding with lots of guests and I went along with that because it was what he wanted and I thought it was what I wanted too. But then I began to get really stressed about the whole thing.

'The day of the wedding dawned; we'd hired a fabulous hotel in London and all our friends and relatives were there. We'd booked a church in the City and it was like a fairy tale. It was my dream come true.

'After all the heartache of discovering that my birth mother wanted nothing to do with me, I so wanted my wedding to be the start of something wonderful. A family life, one that I'd made for myself, was the most important thing to me at that time.

'I arrived at the church wearing the most magnificent dress, carrying a stunningly gorgeous bouquet of lilies and roses. But there was no Oliver. He should have been there before me but neither he nor the best man had arrived.

'So there I was, in my white satin dress, on what should have been the happiest day of my life, but the one person who should have been with me hadn't turned up. Then, just as my car was about to take another turn around the block, the best man arrived and rushed over to tell me that Oliver couldn't go through with it. It was as simple as that. In one tiny moment all the pictures I'd had of the rest of my life turned to dust.

'I felt as if I couldn't breathe; my hands became damp with sweat and I found myself having a major panic attack which was followed by my spending weeks alone in my flat. I didn't even see Oliver when he came to pick up his things. Once or twice, old friends have told me they've seen him and that he's told them how sorry he is about what he did and that he wants to make it up to me. Since he left me in the lurch, none of his other relation-ships have come to anything.

'But at least he's been able to form other relationships, while I haven't been out with another man since. There's too much at stake for me. Do you see what I'm trying to tell you, Adam?'

'I realise that you need to be treated like fine porcelain because of the terrible way you were treated by Oliver.'

'He did let me down badly. And it was Sarah, bless her, who — despite being a bit of a handful herself at times — came and rescued me. She insisted I try a completely different career, that I get away from the City. It was her idea that I should take the money I'd earned in bonuses and start up a business. She was right; it was my salvation. But, well, Adam, I wanted you to know all this because . . .'

'Because what?'

'Because you kissed me the other evening, and you're the first person I've allowed to get that close to me since Oliver left.' She couldn't read the expression on his face. But when she said, 'And I'm afraid of letting you get any closer,' he seemed to stiffen and grow cold.

'I see,' he said.

Did he see? Did he understand that she was trying to say that she knew it meant nothing to him when he held her hand and when he kissed her? That as long as he was able to flirt with other women like Jemini, he was seriously off limits. Cassandra couldn't let him get under her skin for the sake of her own self-preservation.

★　★　★

They gathered up their picnic things and went silently back to the car.

'I appreciate your letting me stay underneath the same roof as you, particularly now that I know how you feel about me.'

How you feel about me. Cassandra sighed inwardly. He'd never know how she really felt about him. Knowing he was spending so much time with Jemini was like a knife going into her. But if she ever told him that she really cared for him and then had to face his rejection, that would be too unbearable.

'Are you taking Jemini out on the boat with you tomorrow?'

'Yes,' he stated simply. Of course he was. They were starting something together, she'd seen it in Jemini's eyes. But Adam's eyes were unreadable at the moment. He looked distant and sad.

She was glad that he went out that evening and didn't return until late.

★ ★ ★

She hadn't been able to sleep until he came in. She heard him moving about in the bathroom, then he slowly opened the bedroom door and crept in.

She lay stock still, feigning sleep but actually acutely conscious of his every move.

She heard Smokey get up from the warm nest he'd made at the end of her bed and jump across to Adam's camp bed, giving a little chirrup.

'Cassandra,' whispered Adam, 'are you asleep?'

She couldn't answer, the lump in her throat would have prevented her from speaking. She couldn't say anything in case she betrayed the fact that that lying alone in her bed with him lying next to her was one of the most difficult things she'd ever done.

★ ★ ★

The next morning, Cassandra made sure she was out of bed and dressed before Adam showed any sign of waking.

She made them both toast, but there was a feeling of tension in the air which hung over the kitchen like a cloud.

'What are your plans for today?' he asked her.

'I've got a builder coming to give me a quote for repairing the ceiling.'

There was a silence, then she said, 'And you're spending a day on the boat, showing Jemini around the bay.'

'That's right. Personally, I think the production company have made a mistake by casting her in the leading role, but the backers feel she's crucial to the success of the whole series. To be honest, she's a spoiled brat and very demanding. It's going to be a long day. Afterwards, we'll be dining at the hotel. The team will need to make up their minds tonight whether or not to use Seaport as their location. It's not up to me to decide, and I don't need to be there, but Jemini's particularly asked that I be at this evening's dinner. She says it's in case there are any questions but really, there have been ample opportunities for me to answer questions these last few days.'

'Well, if you don't have a choice then you'll have to go. You'd better be careful you don't get sunburned on the boat, though. It's going to be a scorcher of a day. I've got some sun cream upstairs you should take with you.'

With that, Cassandra quickly finished her breakfast and busied herself with clearing away.

★ ★ ★

The whole of the day, she couldn't help thinking what a great time Adam and

Jemini must have been having out on the boat.

Her mind simply wasn't on the lunch time customers. Every time she glanced through the window and caught a glimpse of the sea glistening in the distance she couldn't help thinking what a gloriously perfect day it was to be out on the water. The sky was bright azure and the sun was the hottest it had been all year.

Jemini would be in her element, in a bright sundress and with her luxuriant hair blowing in the breeze. The thought made Cassandra's skin prickle.

'Are you feeling all right?' Megan's kind words entered her consciousness. 'You look awful, as if you've eaten something that didn't agree with you.'

'I'm fine,' lied Cassandra. She hadn't even asked Adam if he'd be back before he went out to dinner tonight.

Surely he'd need to freshen up after a day out on the sea?

She found herself throwing stuff into the dishwasher so angrily that Jorge put a hand on her shoulder and told her to leave the plates on the side so he could do it. The sooner Adam was out of her life the better, she thought bitterly. For the first time since he'd arrived, she genuinely wished he would go.

★ ★ ★

It was three o'clock, and everything had been cleared away after lunch when a taxi cab pulled up outside the Feng Shui. Cassandra glanced up, wondering whether they could delay closing. If it was a party of four for a late lunch, she'd hate to turn them away. Then she realised it was Adam, on his own.

But there seemed to be something wrong with him. Instead of being full of energy as usual, he had his head bowed and the taxi driver appeared to be helping him out of the car and towards the restaurant. Had he hurt himself in some way?

She rushed out, just as Adam staggered on to the pavement.

'What's wrong?' Her imploring look questioned first Adam, then the taxi driver who seemed very concerned.

'A nasty case of sunstroke, I think,' said the driver. 'I'm no doctor, but I had it myself once. Felt ghastly I did. The room kept swimming around like I'd had a skinful and yet I hadn't had a drop to drink. Every time I tried to get up, I just collapsed again. It's horrid. You should get him to drink lots of fluid and take it easy.'

Cassandra helped the driver to get Adam to a chair inside the restaurant, and she couldn't help but notice how much Adam's hand was shaking as he paid his fare.

After she'd closed the door and put up the *CLOSED* sign, she pulled him out of the chair, and put his arm around her shoulder.

'Oh Lord, look at the back of your neck, it's bright red. I should have told you to wear a hat or at least made you tie a scarf round your neck. How could you have been so stupid?'

'Quite easily. I seem to be making a habit of it, lately.' Adam leaned heavily on her and managed to get one foot after the other up the stairs.

'I feel like I'm going to die.'

'Well, you're not. You're just gong to feel pretty ghastly for a day or so. Here get yourself into the bed.'

'No, I'll take the camp bed, I can't kick you out of your own bed.'

'Don't be ridiculous.' Cassandra felt a tug at her heartstrings that he could feel concern for her even when he was so ill. 'Just lie down on the bed and stretch out.'

A Visitor From The Past

As Adam groaned and complained that the room was spinning, she carefully undid his shoes, took off his socks and shirt, then laid him carefully back down.

'My head feels like there's someone in there with a hammer.'

'I'll get you some aspirin.'

She rushed off to fetch the aspirins and a large bottle of fizzy water from the restaurant fridge.

'Here,' she said, propping his head up on her arm. 'Take these and drink lots of water.'

Throughout the afternoon, she placed a succession of cool flannels on his forehead and found a fan at the back of one of the cupboards which she put in the corner of the bedroom. Every fifteen minutes she went up to check on him and to make him sip a little more water. Finally, he slipped into a deep sleep. When she went up at six o'clock to check on him, she found him sitting on the side of the bed.

'What are you doing?'

'I've got to get up.' He held his head as if it might fall off if he didn't.

'But you're not well enough.'

'I have to get to that dinner.'

As he rose, he teetered dizzily and fell backwards on to the mattress.

Cassandra lifted his legs and put him straight back into bed again.

'You're far too ill, Adam. You'll be sick if you try to get up and in any case, you said yourself you don't need to be there. Surely if you explain to Jemini how ill you are she'll understand. In fact, she'll probably be so worried that she'll want to come here and see how you are.'

He gave Cassandra a strange look. 'I'm not sure Jemini's the sort of girl who'd take much to nursing, although she did have a part as a nurse once.'

At least he hadn't lost his sense of humour.

She thought how difficult it would be for her if Jemini did come to visit Adam but, as long as he got better, she didn't care.

'Could you possibly get my mobile for me, it's in the top pocket of my jacket?'

Cassandra fetched the mobile for him, then straightened up the bed and poured him some more water.

She heard Jemini's voice down the phone as he was trying to explain his predicament and it didn't sound as if the other woman was overcome with loving care, more as if she was telling him off.

'I really can't come tonight, Jemini, I've got horrendous sunstroke. I feel awful . . . '

Cassandra could see his jaw tightening. He didn't need this.

'I would get there if I could, Jemini, you know that. Yes, I know you were looking forward to it, and I know how important it is to you to have me there but — '

He closed his eyes, then put the phone down on the bedside table.

'She's hung up on me.'

Cassandra wanted to pick up the phone, call Jemini back, and give her a piece of her mind.

'Will this affect the outcome of their decision?'

For once she found herself wanting Adam to succeed in his project. He'd worked so hard at it.

'I don't know, it doesn't look good though. Jemini's furious with me. She got very friendly, or rather, tried to, this afternoon. The closer she got, the more I tried to move away but there aren't many places to run to on a boat. She's unused to men who don't give her their full attention.' He groaned, settling back on his pillow. 'All I know right now is that you're here and that means a lot to me.'

Cassandra flushed pink and turned away so that he couldn't see the sadness in her eyes. He might be here with Cassandra and he may have tried to cool Jemini's ardour on the boat but the fact still remained that if he hadn't been ill he'd be sitting next to Jemini at dinner right now.

'I'd better go downstairs. We've a lot of bookings tonight.' As she looked back, she realised he'd already fallen into a slumber.

As she served dinner to the guests in the restaurant, she turned Adam's words over and over in her mind. *Had* he rejected Jemini? Was that why she was so cross with him? But Jemini was such a catch, most men would have fallen at her feet. Maybe Cassandra had misjudged Adam; maybe he hadn't fallen for the actress's shallow charms.

★   ★   ★

The whole of the next day, she kept check on him, making sure he drank plenty of fluids and rested. When he was well enough, she propped him up with cushions and gave him something to eat.

By the evening, he had recovered enough to come down and have a light supper in the restaurant. That evening, there was a barbecue at the music festival and bookings were very low.

'I think I need some fresh air; it's such a beautiful evening. As my nurse, would you consider taking me down just as far as the harbour and back again?'

'Of course I will. I think we could both do with a change of scene.'

They walked past a line of boats with multicoloured sails and watched a cruise ship dock in the harbour, then they leaned against the seawall and watched the last of the sunset.

'Cassandra, I want to thank you for looking after me.'

'It was nothing.'

How could he know it had been sheer pleasure for her to have him there?

'I've been thinking, Adam. I've been very selfish trying to stop the filming coming to Seaport. You've put everything into your project and I mustn't be so closed-minded. It *could* bring benefits. I just want you to know that I hope the decision is positive for you and that you have my blessing.'

He turned towards her, the last rays of the sun glinting on the water and said, 'That means a huge amount to me. I think, whatever happens, that you're stronger than you think. You could cope with anything Cassandra, and make a success of anything.'

Except relationships, she thought, quaking inside about what tomorrow might bring. If the decision was made not to film here, then there would be no reason for Adam to come to Seaport again.

'It's time we went back. You mustn't tire yourself out.'

'I guess you're right. You're the best nurse a guy could have.'

Nurse, landlady, cook but nothing more, thought Cassandra.

And that was the last thought that went through her head as she settled down in her bed that night, and lay near Adam who'd insisted on taking the camp bed again. She heard him turn over on to his side and sigh.

There was so much she wanted to say to him, but maybe it was better this way, safer, and she must relish just having him here at least for one night longer.

★　★　★

The next day, just as they'd sat down to breakfast, the hotel had phoned to tell Adam that, if he was still interested, they had several spare rooms available. There was now no reason for him to stay at the restaurant and so he was upstairs packing his bag.

With a heaviness in her footsteps, Cassandra went to pick up the post from the mat and was surprised to find a letter addressed to Adam amongst the mail.

She ran up and left it on the landing table so that he would see it when he came out of his room after he'd finished getting his things ready.

When there was a knock at the restaurant door, she thought it might be the postman returning with a forgotten letter or parcel and she rushed to open it, the wind catching it and almost knocking her over.

If she'd looked up at the sky, she'd have noticed the billowing grey clouds that heralded the storm that was about to break the long run of warm hot weather. The leaves in the trees seemed to whisper and wave to each other to watch out. Today was going to be wild and wet.

But she wasn't looking up at the sky as she opened the restaurant door, and thoughts about the weather were the last thing on her mind because the sight of the man who stood before her, in a crisp charcoal suit and immaculate white shirt, shocked her to the core. The one person she had never expected to see again stood in front of her.

'Oliver!'

'Cassandra. I'm sorry to turn up like

this without warning. I should have phoned but I was frightened you might refuse to see me.'

'I'd never turn away an old friend, Oliver. You look well.'

Amazed at her own sudden composure she found she was on autopilot, as if she was listening to someone else speak.

'I can see I've caught you by surprise. I'll go away if it's a bad time.'

'No, no come in. I'm sorry, for someone who owns a restaurant I'm not being very hospitable. Would you care for a coffee?'

'That would be lovely. I'm here on business, Cassandra, my company's financing a new multimillion pound venture at the docks in Frederickstowe. When I was first assigned the job, I couldn't stop thinking that it was near where you lived and I'm afraid I came on impulse. The car almost brought me here on its own.'

She poured coffee for the two of them, struggling to keep her hand steady. As she did so, her back tensed as she heard footsteps coming down the stairs. Turning around, she saw first surprise, then recognition pass over Adam's face as he put down his bag at the bottom of the stairs.

'I hope I'm not interrupting anything.'

Oliver cast a glance at Cassandra, trying to read from her face who this person might be.

He got up and held out a hand. 'Oliver Crossland.'

'Adam Hawthorne.'

There was no, 'Pleased to meet you,' on either side. The men appeared to have observed the conventions of politeness only because, being gentlemen, they had to.

'I'll be on my way now, Cassandra,' said Adam. His tone was low, like thunder, matching the gathering turbulence outside. 'I just have to get my laptop.'

As he disappeared back up the stairs, Cassandra turned to Oliver and said,

'Excuse me. Mr Hawthorne's been renting the spare room. I must just go and check that he's taken all his belongings with him.'

She ran up the stairs as quickly as her feet would carry her. 'Adam, I just wanted to explain. The man downstairs, he's — '

'I know who he is, Cassandra, you've told me all about him. He's your ex-fiancé, isn't he?' Adam's tones were clipped, his voice flat. As he spoke, fat drops of rain spotted the window.

'Yes. He's just turned up out of the blue. He's here on business. I'm sure he won't be staying.' *He doesn't mean anything to me*, she wanted to add, but Adam was being so brusque.

'I don't want to crowd you out, Cassandra. I was leaving anyway.'

Stiffly, he held out a hand and shook hers as if they were strangers.

Then, as if regretting his coldness, and remembering his caring side he said, 'You will be OK won't you? It must be a bit of a shock having someone from the past turn up like this unexpectedly.'

'I'm fine, Adam. It all seems like a very long time ago now. Oliver is like a stranger to me.'

Adam seemed unmoved, set in his desire to leave. Something other than Oliver arriving had happened this morning; she could see it weighing on his mind, causing troubled lines to develop on his brow.

'Take care of yourself.'

As he made his way down the stairs, she wanted to ask how long he'd be staying at the hotel in Seaport; when she'd see him again; whether he'd fully recovered. But it was all so difficult with Oliver there. All she managed at the door was, 'Goodbye,' such an inadequate expression of how sad she was to see him go.

Oliver didn't seem to notice how downcast she'd become; being sensitive to other people's moods was not one of his strong points.

'That wind is pretty brisk.' He walked

over to the door and closed it for her. 'Sit down, Cassandra, and tell me how you've been. I don't know if you've been able to forgive me, yet? And there's so much I need to say to you. But the main thing is, I've missed you.'

He sat down opposite her, trying to read her enigmatic expression.

★　★　★

This was a bolt from the blue after so long! Weeks ago, before Adam had come on the scene, Cassandra might have melted to hear those words. They would have turned her inside out, but now she felt a thousand times stronger.

Getting to know Adam had changed her.

The realisation came like a beam of light.

She watched the crystals in the window send glittering sparkles dancing around the restaurant.

'Do you see those crystals hanging in the window, Oliver?'

He looked mystified. 'Yes.'

'I've learned so much since you and I split up, about how I want to live my life and about what's important to me. When I hung those crystals there a few months ago, I told myself I'd done it just because they were pretty.'

'They are. I really like what you've done with this place.'

'But you don't understand any of the principles of Feng Shui. Crystals hung in that part of a room are designed to bring romance into a life. That's what I was looking for all along.'

'We had that, didn't we?' He reached over the table.

She leaned away from him. 'We did, Oliver, but I don't think you and I ever really had anything that would last. We lived in a frantic world where we wanted the best of everything. We worked hard and played hard but everything was superficial. I was devastated when you left me, absolutely distraught. I thought I'd lost everything. But look at me now. I've built

270

this place up from scratch. The pace of life is slower here but it means so much more. But as well as that, I think I've met someone who means a lot to me, and who might need me more than you ever did.'

She tipped her head at an angle and looked questioningly at him.

'Why did you come here today?'

He shuffled uncomfortably in his seat. 'I suppose I'm looking for something, too. Things have been very empty since you and I split. I think about that day a lot. I was very immature then. I didn't think my actions through. I got frightened by the whole marriage thing and I just ran away. I've had a lot of time to think since we split and my thoughts always turn to you. Could you ever forgive me, Cassandra? Could we ever try again? I wouldn't crowd you, we could start again slowly.'

The question hung in the air. It seemed to fill the restaurant. Rain was now lashing at the windows and trickling down the glass. She didn't know how to answer.

Suddenly there was a knock at the door which startled her out of her thoughts and there, standing on the step, rain dripping off her spiky hair, was Sarah, looking happier and more radiant than Cassandra had seen her in a long time.

'Sorry I took so long to come back and get my stuff. I hope it wasn't in your way. Is it OK if I stay a few days? Oops, I didn't realise you had someone with you.'

Sarah had crashed in through the door, not noticing anyone else as she rushed in to get out of the rain.

'Oliver!' She looked even more shocked than Cassandra had. But Sarah's capacity to forgive wasn't as great as her sister's and her face lost its smile as she said, blatantly hostile, 'What are you doing here?'

'I think I'd better leave you two girls to it. Here, Cassandra, this is my card with my mobile number on it. Please phone me. Maybe we could go out for a drink. I'd really like to continue our conversation.'

'I'll phone you.' Cassandra watched from the door as Oliver clambered into a sleek black Volvo. Firing up the engine he gave her a wistful smile as he drove past, fixing his gaze on her for as long as he could before disappearing from view.

Everything about him screamed money and status and reminded her so much of her past shallow life that she shuddered as she shut the door.

* * *

When she turned around, deep in thought, wearily tucking a stray lock of hair back into her ponytail, her sister had flopped down on to one of the restaurant chairs.

Cassandra patted a pile of clean white napkins that stood on the side counter, and looked at the silver cutlery all shining and in its correct place. So much that she'd achieved here was perfect, but there was just one thing missing.

The fact that she had no-one to share it with.

'Wow, you look as if you've had a heavy morning!'

'Not just a heavy morning, the last few days have been pretty trying.'

She related the events of the past few days to her open-mouthed sister, telling her all about the collapsed ceiling, sharing a room with Adam, Adam's illness and the fact that today was the day they would hear whether or not the filming was to go ahead in Seaport.

'The way you talk about Adam I would say he's the one you should be thinking of phoning, not Oliver.'

Sarah leant over and took her sister's hands in hers. 'Please tell me you're not thinking about getting back together with Oliver. Please tell me that after all this time you're not going to let him waltz back into your life as if nothing has happened.'

'Oh, no. I think I can see that Oliver hasn't changed but I know I have. The thing is ... I ... I think ... Oh, heavens, I don't just think it, I know it! I'm in love with Adam.'

'Hey, Cass, that's great.'

'It isn't great! Not really. I'm convinced that he and Jemini Devane have a thing going, and why on earth would he look twice at me with her around?'

'You know something, Cass? They say love is blind but you're just standing there looking the other way. Haven't you seen the way he watches you? And you say he's been staying here. It isn't just because there aren't any hotel rooms. He could easily find somewhere up the coast; he's got a car, hasn't he? He's stayed here because he couldn't keep away from you. In the same way he can't keep his eyes off you whenever you're in the room. I've seen him; why you can't see it for yourself, I don't know!'

'Oh, I wish you were right, Sarah.'

'Trust me. I may not be the one with the business brain and I may be rubbish with money and I may struggle to hold down a job. But I'm right about this, Cass! Why don't you get straight on that phone to the hotel and speak to him? Be honest with him and be honest with yourself. You're good at taking risks in business. For once, take a risk in your personal life.'

*   *   *

Sarah took her sister's hand, marched her upstairs and positioned her firmly in front of the phone. Handing her the receiver, she said, 'Go for it! Give the hotel a ring. And just so you can have a little privacy, I'm not going to be nosy for once. I'll go and put a towel over my wet hair and get my bag sorted and wait in the spare room until you've finished.'

Her hand trembling, Cassandra dialled the number of the hotel.

'Mr Adam Hawthorne? I'm afraid

276

he hasn't re-booked his room here. He certainly isn't staying here tonight. In fact, his party have all left the hotel. As far as I know, they were going back to London.'

Where Is Adam?

Back to London? As Cassandra put down the phone, she felt she was moving in slow motion. Sarah came out of the bedroom cradling Smokey in her arms. The kitten was playing with one of the buttons on her denim jacket.

In her hand she held a letter which was crumpled and creased as if it had been screwed up and thrown away.

'I found this on the spare room floor. I think you should read it.'

It was a letter to Adam from Jed Michaels. With profuse apologies, he explained that he'd decided to delay a decision on the TV series. He said that most of the production team liked Adam's choice of location, but that Jemini Devane had raised various objections and they were reviewing the whole project.

'What does that mean, I wonder?'

Cassandra was mystified. 'Everything seemed to be going so well for Adam, and he's put so much effort in. I was sure they were going to go for his plan.'

'You know what I reckon?' Sarah stroked Smokey's head. 'I reckon Jemini's nose was put out of joint by the fact that Adam wasn't going to jump to her beck and call. She sounds like a little madam who wants everything her own way. People like her play mind games as soon as they get a bit of success, and they want to run other people's lives. The last few days must have been pretty hellish for Adam.'

'They must have been. And I feel so bad about having made objections to the filming in the first place. I went into a complete whirl and suspected all the TV people of being like Jemini, self-centred and domineering. In fact, Jed Michaels and Ann Somer, the producer, were lovely people. I could kick myself for judging the situation before I'd met them. I'd be surprised if Adam ever wanted to see me again. I've ruined his chances.'

Sarah placed Smokey down on the floor, smoothing his velvety grey fur and eliciting a chirrup of pleasure from him, then she straightened up and enfolded her sister in her arms.

'Cass, I've never seen you looking so down. You've got so much on your plate at the moment. But everything'll be all right, you'll see. You said the builder's coming today to repair the ceiling, didn't you? Let me stay on and help you out the way you helped me when I needed it.

'I can start by offering to oversee the builder — it'll only take him a day to re-plaster in the bedroom, then I can help out in the restaurant if you want and we'll paint the bedroom together once the plaster's dry.

'What you should concentrate on is trying to find Adam and, when you do, be honest with him about how you feel. Do you have his mobile number?'

'I do, but — '

'But nothing! Be brave, Cass, I know

it's difficult, but I don't want to see you turning down the chance of something really special. Maybe Oliver turning up here today wasn't just a coincidence. I believe in fate and I think he turned up at just the right time to show you what's important to you and to remind you that, actually, you had a lucky escape when he left. Please?' She gave Cassandra the phone. 'Ring Adam's mobile.'

★ ★ ★

But when Cassandra dialled the number it kept diverting her to a messaging service. She didn't want to leave a message; what could she say that would be appropriate? She needed to speak to him.

'I'll try later, Sarah, I promise I will.'

'Cass, you've always been the strong one, the sensible one. But, for a change, it's my turn to sort you out. What's the point of you not leaving Adam a message? For heaven's sake, give the poor man a clue about the fact that you care for him. I know it goes against the grain with you; I can see it in your face that you don't think that's cool and that it's taking too much of a chance with your emotions. But look at me. You know I wear my heart on my sleeve. Sometimes that's fatal, I'll admit. But sometimes it works. It worked with me and Dave. Phone Adam again. Leave a message. Trust me this once.'

Cassandra picked up the phone again and, composing a message carefully in her head, she pushed the buttons.

This time, when Adam's recorded voice came on the line again, she spoke, leaving a simple but heartfelt message asking him to get in touch with her as soon as he could and telling him that she missed him.

'That should do it,' said Sarah. 'If he doesn't respond to that pretty quickly, then I've misjudged him. But I can't believe I have. I have a feeling deep down about you two.'

Three days passed and there was no word from Adam. As each day ticked by, Cassandra became more down-hearted.

The storm that had been brewing on the day he'd left had presaged several days of solid rain.

It spattered in the streets outside the Feng Shui and flowed down the gutters in endless dirty rivulets.

The weather mirrored her mood but she tried to stay positive. She smiled at her customers, joked with Jorge — trying to make him laugh the way that Adam had — and put on a brave face when Sarah kept asking, 'Are you OK?'

Taking her sister's advice, she'd left three other messages for Adam.

Just hearing his voice was heaven to her, even though over and over, all she heard was, 'Hi, it's Adam, please leave a message,' before the inevitable click and silence.

He wasn't going to answer, and she

didn't blame him.

Why would he ever want to speak again to the woman who had completely fouled up a lucrative business plan?

Now she regretted every negative word she'd uttered about the filming.

Over and over again she thought of how he'd helped her when her car had broken down, how he'd laughed at her, good-naturedly, at the boot fair for being so naïve in her dealings with all the sharp dealers.

She thought longingly of the way he'd got on so well with her customers, and how he'd charmed Jorge and, above all, she remembered those leisurely walks on the beach; the time he'd held her hand; the way he'd kissed her.

But she'd been so prickly and suspicious of him and now she had only herself to blame that he wasn't coming back.

★ ★ ★

One Saturday, in an effort to cheer up her sister and pull her out of her quiet desperation, Sarah had insisted Cassandra take the afternoon off to go and have lunch with Ellie.

Ellie had arranged to meet her at the local bistro, and Cassandra knew she should have dressed up a little. It would have done her good, maybe lifted her spirits, to have fussed over what she was going to wear, but instead she had pulled on a plain navy shift dress and used a plain navy ribbon to hold back her ponytail.

She could hardly be bothered these days to put on make-up, but she made herself flick a bit of mascara on her eyelashes, as much as anything to hide her eyes which lately gave in too easily to tears.

Finally, she made herself put on a pair of simple pearl drop earrings.

Even her skin looked tired, but the pearls helped to lighten the outfit.

At least it wasn't raining that day, although the sky was still grey and leaden and threatening.

As she pushed through the doors of the estate agent's, Cassandra stopped in her tracks. There was Ann Somer sitting opposite Ellie! What on earth could she be doing there? She'd only once met the producer — at that fateful dinner in her restaurant — but Cassandra had liked Ann; liked her honesty and her no nonsense attitude.

'Hi, Ann, how are you?'

'I'm very well, thank you. But I'm afraid I might be in danger of crashing in on your lunch with Ellie here.'

'That's right,' said Ellie grabbing her bag and coat. 'If it's all right with you, Cassie, Ann's going to join us. The thing is, she's fallen in love with Seaport. I sent her some details of properties and she's thinking of buying a weekend retreat in the area. She wants to know about the best places to buy and, as you went through all of this when you bought the restaurant, I thought it would be good to give her the client's point of view as well as mine as an estate agent.'

'That's fine by me,' Cassandra said as they left Ellie's office and crossed the road to the bistro.

★ ★ ★

Over their lunch, they discussed various property options in the area, but at the back of Cassandra's mind was the need to know whether Ann had had any contact with Adam.

Ann obviously had no idea how Cassandra felt about Adam, and Cassandra was grateful when — once they'd finished discussing the merits of the harbour area over the beach area — Ellie asked the producer, 'So, have you seen any of the other TV people lately?'

Ann had just finished off her steak au poivre. 'Well, I probably shouldn't be telling you this, but Jed and I have been talking and we've decided that the project is a strong enough one to go ahead without Jemini.'

'Without her?' Cassandra suddenly perked up.

'Absolutely. It was Jed's idea to pursue her because she's the flavour of the moment but, frankly, the girl's a complete disaster. She's about the most controlling, conceited little madam I've ever come across. It's girls like her who give actresses a bad name. Do you know, in a typical fit of pique, she threw Adam Hawthorne's mobile phone into the sea?'

'What?' Cassandra felt a glimmer of hope begin to bubble in her heart.

'Absolutely. That day on the boat was a nightmare. Adam did his best to keep everything businesslike and all she did was keep on fluttering her eyelashes at him. I could see him getting more and more annoyed with her because he wanted her to concentrate on discussing different sites for filming. After all, she was the one who had suggested the boat tour. I'm sure she'd wanted to be on her own with him but he'd insisted that Jed and I go, too, and once I was there, I could see why. She's a real man-eater that girl, but Adam was having none of it.'

Cassandra couldn't believe her ears. She'd got it so wrong. 'But I thought he was keen on her? He was so nice to her at that dinner in my restaurant.'

'I'm afraid, Cassandra, that in our business you have to flatter actors and actresses. You have to pretend they are the centre of the universe. Poor Adam! She drove him too far. On the boat trip, she insisted the boat should cruise endlessly up and down the coast even though the sun was vicious. Jed and I sat in the shade and dozed off, but she insisted on Adam staying with her up on deck. It was all right for her, she had on a huge sunhat and shades. She should never have pressured him like that. I'm not surprised he got sunstroke, poor thing. Still, I got hold of him today with a bit of good news.'

Cassandra leaned forward in her seat, pushing her half-eaten lunch away. 'You spoke to him today?'

'Yes. I'm afraid you're not going to like what I said to him, Cassandra.'

'Why not?'

'Well, I sort of engineered this lunch with you and Ellie! I have absolutely fallen in love with Seaport. I think it's the ideal location for the series and I've managed to sign up a different actress who is much less a soap star and more a serious actress for the lead role. We are coming here to film and I've asked Adam to come down today to sign the contract for all the location planning. I'm sorry if that's bad news? I know you didn't want the filming to go ahead here.'

Cassandra felt her throat go dry. Adam was coming back to Seaport today!

'I didn't, but I've realised I was wrong, and very selfish. I'm actually really pleased for you and for Adam. He was right, it is a lovely location and I was stupid to get so worked up about it. I'm actually proud to live here and proud to think people will get to know it more. When did you say you were going to see Adam?'

'Shortly, at the hotel. I said I'd meet him in the bar after lunch. Why don't you come along?'

'I . . .' Cassandra thought for a second. Her heart had somersaulted when she'd heard that he had simply lost his mobile rather than been ignoring her calls.

But would he want to see her again? He could have contacted her if he'd wanted to. She'd been at the Feng Shui the whole time. If he hadn't got in touch it must be because he didn't want to. He must blame her for putting his project at risk.

'No, it's very kind of you, but I'll be busy at the restaurant this afternoon. In fact, I'd better be getting back there now.'

It was a lie. Sarah had told her to take the afternoon off. But she couldn't eat any more, couldn't even think straight, her mind was such a complete jumble. She needed to get away somewhere quiet.

★   ★   ★

Once they'd said goodbye to Ann, Ellie caught her friend by the arm. 'Are you sure you're all right, Cassandra? You look so pale.'

Cassandra told her about Oliver's visit, and about the fact that she'd decided to phone him and tell him she couldn't see him again. She knew he wasn't the one for her and seeing him again would only open up old wounds. But what of Adam?

'I'm going to take a walk, Ellie, down by the sea. I need to think.'

She made her way down to the sea front as if she was on automatic pilot. It was only a short walk along the shore to reach the two lighthouses. As she picked her way over pebbles and shells towards the soft damp sand, she looked out at the grey sea and she clasped her warm coat around her, marvelling at the difference a few days made.

Such a short time ago things had

been so sunny, so bright; there had been a million possibilities and now there were none.

The wind blew in her ears, whipping her ponytail back and forth so that the ribbon worked its way out of her hair and tumbled across the sand.

She stumbled after it, feeling beaten and battered by the weather, and by all that the last few weeks had thrown at her.

The wind was growing stronger now; it scooped up grains of sand that stung her face. She closed her eyes as she stumbled along the shoreline, only half-seeing where she was going, vainly pursuing the ribbon that danced mockingly away from her like tumbleweed in a gale. It was hopeless. Everything seemed hopeless.

'Is this what you were running after, Cassandra?'

Eyes still stinging from the sand, she turned her back to the wind, her hair swirling wildly about her face. The familiar voice sounded so much like

Adam's. Then she felt strong, comforting, familiar hands take her hair in a long skein and tie the ribbon back on. When her unruly locks had been tamed, she rubbed her eyes, opening them to see Adam standing before her, his denim collar pulled up against the wind.

'Adam! What are you doing here?'

'I met at Ann at the hotel. She told me she'd seen you. She also told me Ellie reckoned you'd head down here for some comfort. Even in this wild weather she says the beach is always your refuge.'

'You're getting soaking wet!' It was a silly thing to say, stating the perfectly obvious as rain poured down from the sky and soaked both of them.

'I don't care.' He took her hand.

'Why did you come back? Was it just because of your work? Where have you been?'

Even in the cold wind and the driving rain, Cassandra felt the warmth of his smile suffuse her like a shot of brandy.

'I came back because I wanted to find you. But I thought you'd taken Oliver back again. I thought that day I saw you together that the two of you were patching things up. Was I wrong?'

'Yes! Oh, yes, you were very wrong. I haven't taken Oliver back again because I don't want him. I don't want his way of life. I . . . I want . . .'

'I know what *I* want, Cassandra. I went away. I took an assignment in Paris for a few days because when I saw you with Oliver I thought there was nothing here for me. Then, when Ann got in touch with me to say it had been decided to restart the project in Seaport, I nearly turned her down. She persuaded me to come back. When I saw her today she told me you suspected I'd had a relationship with Jemini Devane and I nearly fell off my seat. I had to come out and find you straight away.'

'There was really nothing between you and Jemini?'

'Nothing but a deep and abiding dislike.' Adam laughed, that deep throaty laugh that Cassandra had feared she might never hear again.

Now she had a feeling she might get to know it much better.

'That woman's a viper. I suspected her of being an arch manipulator right from the start. I could never have worked with her. It was always you I wanted, Cassandra, but I still felt so guilty about Jenny's death. I felt it would be disloyal . . . I tried to send you signals but I never knew if you cared or whether you wanted to be alone forever.'

'No, Adam, I don't want to be alone.'

'Then make a new start with me, Cassandra. Here, in Seaport.'

He bent down, ran his thumb across her lips to remove the rain drops, then stroked her wet hair while he brought his mouth down on to hers.

For a long time they stood together on the deserted beach with the wind whipping around them and the rain

mixed with sea spray lashing against
them.

But all Cassandra could feel was
Adam protecting her from the elements
and she knew she had never felt warmer
in her whole life.

THE END

We do hope that you have enjoyed reading this large print book.

Did you know that all of our titles are available for purchase?

We publish a wide range of high quality large print books including:
Romances, Mysteries, Classics
General Fiction
Non Fiction and Westerns

Special interest titles available in large print are:
The Little Oxford Dictionary
Music Book, Song Book
Hymn Book, Service Book

Also available from us courtesy of Oxford University Press:
Young Readers' Dictionary
(large print edition)
Young Readers' Thesaurus
(large print edition)

For further information or a free brochure, please contact us at:
Ulverscroft Large Print Books Ltd.,
The Green, Bradgate Road, Anstey,
Leicester, LE7 7FU, England.
Tel: (00 44) **0116 236 4325**
Fax: (00 44) **0116 234 0205**